Praise for

Therefore I Have Hope

"*Therefore I Have Hope* is a tender story that explores the importance of family, restoration, and forgiveness. A gentle reminder that no matter how far away we might be from those we love or from the Lord, He will always lead us back to Him. *Therefore I Have Hope* is a lovely story."

- CAITLIN MILLER, author of *The Memories We Painted* and *Our Yellow Tape Letters*

"The nostalgia was strong with this one! *Therefore I Have Hope* is a charming story with a delectable retro vibe and powerful themes of perseverance and restoration that will uplift readers of all ages!"

- GRACE A. JOHNSON, author of the *Daughters of the Seven Seas* series

THEREFORE

I HAVE

HOPE

THEREFORE

I HAVE

HOPE

Daisy Henkle

Mau Loa Publishers

Therefore I Have Hope

Copyright © 2023 by Daisy Henkle

Mau Loa Publishers

Scripture quotations are taken from the *Holy Bible,* New King James Version.

ISBN: 979-8-218-29219-5

Cover design: Adobe Firefly with additional edits by the author

Hope itself is like a star – not to be seen in the

sunshine of prosperity, and only to be discovered

in the night of adversity.

~Charles H. Spurgeon

CHAPTER ONE
TIM

I've never been much for dances.

I watch from a corner of the Greenfield Community High School gym as colorful, flashing lights illuminate a banner which reads: Back to School Dance, 1986. My eyes shift downwards and land on my friend Matt Williams, who's performing with his band. The electric sound of their music is echoing and bouncing around the room, sending an excited sort of energy into everyone present.

Matt's forehead is glistening as he plays a riff on his guitar, and he wipes it hastily with the back of his hand and continues playing, his dark hair falling over his eyes. You'd think he'd be nervous to sing and play guitar in front of the whole school, but he's not. Matt was born to do this. Me, on the other hand? Not a chance. I prefer standing on the sidelines. Matt likes to say I'm his unofficial manager, but nothing I've done has helped his band get to where they are today - which is, like I said, them performing at a school dance.

The gym is mostly dark, the shimmering reflection of a disco ball supplying most of the light in the room. That's fine by me; if someone saw me, they might try to get me to dance, and I'm not in the mood. Usually, my only reason for coming to these dances is to be Matt's moral support.

1

The band rings out the final note of "Danger Zone," and Matt hands the guitar over to his friend Kevin, who begins playing "The Heat Is On." Jumping off the side of the platform, he makes his way over to me through the crowd, a couple inches shorter than me now that he isn't elevated by the stage.

"So, manager," he says, crossing his arms and leaning against the wall, "how was that?"

I shrug and scratch my head of light caramel-colored hair. "Well, I did see a few people sneak out the back…"

Matt's grin stretches from ear to ear, and he shakes his head. "Hey, that's better than last time."

I laugh and take a sip from the can of 7UP in my hand. Without warning, Matt elbows me in the side, and I almost drop my can, unable to keep some of the soda from splashing onto the right sleeve of my shirt. "What the heck?"

"You really should be a part of the band," says Matt earnestly.

With a long groan, I shake my head and reach over to the snack table to grab a napkin to dry my shirt. "Haven't I told you a thousand times? No can do. I'll be your manager as long as you want, but I'm not getting on any stage."

"But you can sing."

"Like a dying cat…"

Matt considers this and then nods in agreement.

"Hey, are we still good for tomorrow…?" Matt's sentence trails off as his eyes land on a girl across the room who's playing with her long, permed hair and absentmindedly staring at the stage. "There's Anne. I gotta bounce. Told her we'd go out tonight." He turns to go, but then stops and looks back at me. "Tim?" His bright blue eyes shift meaningfully over to a blonde-haired girl I've met once (whose name I think is Julie) who is standing next to Anne.

Shaking my head in amusement, I gesture towards his girlfriend. "Not my type. Get outta here."

Matt raises his eyebrows in disapproval. Suddenly, his eyes light up, and he snaps his fingers. "Hey, I just re-membered, I think you owe me five -"

I dig into my pocket and slap a five-dollar bill (fresh from my paper route pay day this morning) into his hand, too used to my friend's antics to be annoyed. "Go, Matt."

With his usual mischievous grin, Matt nods and final-ly takes off, his old white and blue Adidas Forums squeaking noisily on the gym floor.

My gaze wanders back up to the stage just as the cur-rent song finishes playing, and Kevin steps towards the mic. "That's all for tonight, people. We'll catch you later."

The crowd begins thinning out, but not quickly. It's almost as if no one wants to leave - but I do. Quickly and quietly, I slip out the gym door and begin making my way down the dimly lit hallway, ready to head home.

I live about ten minutes away from school, driving distance. I got my license a year ago, but my foster parents, the Fishers, almost never let me use their car. Today is one of those rare occasions where I'm permitted to use it. Somehow, I don't think the Fishers are very keen on a newer driver using their car - even if I am a senior who's had his license an entire year. I can't really blame them, but it's not as if I've ever been irresponsible around them. Anyways, had they said no, I would have just ridden my bike tonight.

I exit out the front doors of the school and spot the Fishers' 1981 Toyota Corolla right away, the light coming from the school reflecting off its shiny gray exterior. It's parked almost directly in front of school, right where I left it. Getting inside, I back out, turn, and begin driving to the house I've had to learn to call home.

A red convertible passes me quickly, playing "Power of Love" by Huey Lewis and the News so loudly that it reminds me of the familiar noise and busyness of my old hometown of Charlotte, North Carolina. But just like that, the car is gone, and so is the noise.

For a guy with my personality, you'd think I'd appreciate the quiet of Greenfield, North Carolina - but I'm accustomed to the sights and sounds of city life. More than once these past few years, I've wished I were still there, where I belong - with the people I used to know. I had lots of friends back in the city. I had a life there. I had - *family* there. I gulp hard.

The streetlight up ahead turns yellow, and I pull to a stop. Reaching down in the back pocket of my jeans, I pull out the familiar, slightly wrinkled photograph of a couple of young boys standing in a park. One is the thirteen-year-old version of me, and the other, a grinning, dark-haired nine-year-old. *My brother.*

Sighing, I tuck the photograph back in my pocket and swallow, my mouth dry. For some reason, I've been thinking about my brother an awful lot lately. But not just him - my parents, too. My old life.

I was fourteen when my parents died in a car crash on August 15th, 1983. About a week after the funeral, it was determined that since I had no family to become my legal guardians, I should be sent to a foster home. I bounced around a bit before landing at the Fishers'. They said this would be good for me, but there was someone else in the mix: my younger brother, Mark.

Due to his "defiant nature," no foster home would keep him for long. That's how we got separated. I, at fourteen years old, and he, at ten, were still shocked, and scared of all the unknowns that lay before us - but being the older one, I couldn't show that. Nah, I never showed it - and if I'm being honest, I'm kinda proud of that fact. So, when we came together one last time to say goodbye, I made him a promise. I promised that one day, I would come back for him.

Well, let's face it: I was only fourteen. I was earnest as I made the promise - but I hadn't thought about every obstacle that I might face in the future that would keep me away from my brother. So, the first year came and went, and I was reminded of the promise, but I was convinced that there was nothing I could do. Besides, the Fishers seemed dead set on helping me adapt to my new life. Whether it was school, sports, or any other activity under the sun, they used every opportunity they could find to try to distract me and relocate my thoughts from Charlotte to Greenfield. They even went as far as to tell me not to respond to my brother's letters. That doesn't really matter, though - I only received one.

After the first few months of my new life in Greenfield, I began feeling desperate to have some peace in my life, so I decided to act like I was completely fine, so that the Fishers wouldn't bother me anymore. They were appeased by the fact that I seemed to have accepted my new life, and I was relieved about that. Compared to my own family, the Fishers are distant at best.

I may not have been able to live a somewhat normal life at all if it weren't for Matt Williams. I met Matt on my first day of school in Greenfield. Like me, he was a freshman, but unlike me, he was one of the most popular guys in school. That's why I was surprised when he volunteered to be my partner in a science project. I remember the very first words he said to me. He had been looking around the room for quite some time, as if trying to decide who to partner up with. Eventually, after having looked from a group of preppy guys on one side of the room to the group of giggling girls on the other, he walked over to me, offered his hand to shake, and said, "You look like the kind of guy who'd be good with blowing stuff up."

It wasn't long before we realized that we didn't have very much in common, him being a loud rock-and-roll-loving, spontaneous troublemaker, and I the responsible, sort of reserved city kid from Charlotte - but at that point in our friendship, it didn't really matter. I just felt lucky that anyone was willing to talk to me, let alone be my friend.

Matt knew from that first week of our friendship that my parents were dead, but I carefully avoided telling him that I had a brother. I'm not totally sure why I did this. I guess I already felt so frustrated - even embarrassed - by my life that I didn't want to give Matt another reason to pity me. I didn't know it then, but avoiding the subject of my brother only added to my newfound ability to gradually forget about him.

CHAPTER TWO
MARK

I hate people.

This is the only thought that goes through my mind as I stand at my bedroom window, looking out at the busy streets of Charlotte, North Carolina. I've lived in this city my whole life, and I've become used to all its sights and sounds; I know it like the back of my hand. This is because of the amount of time I've spent just observing things - and that's also how I learned how much I hate people.

I watch as a traffic jam begins, and people start to press down on their horns. I almost scoff at the sight of them all; in my mind, they're all just impatient, angry people who have nothing better to do than get frustrated with one another.

Hearing a small shuffling noise, I turn away from the window and am faced by blond-haired, grinning Ben Robinson, one of the three boys I share a room with at the Bentwood Foster Home.

"Hey," he says quietly with a little nod. I don't reply; I simply nod back and continue standing at the window. I watch as Ben sits down on his twin-sized bed, kicks back, and grabs a book from the small nightstand that sits in between his bed and mine.

Suddenly, Ben looks up and sees me watching him. With a smile, he holds up the book for me to see. "It's called *Ender's Game*. It just came out last year."

I merely nod again and stuff my hands into the pockets of my jeans.

Undeterred, Ben presses on. "Well, want to read it? It's super good. I've only got a couple pages left. I bet you'd like it."

I lean against the wall and shake my head of dark brown hair.

Ben shrugs. "Suit yourself."

I stare down at my dirty Converse as Ben goes back to his book. Eventually, though, I look up slowly and see the way Ben's eyes are widening as he turns a page. Truthfully, I *do* want to read the book - it's better than having nothing to do at all. But the way my head has been hurting lately, I'm not sure I could focus long enough to read a whole book.

What I *really* want is to go outside and play a game, like baseball or basketball. I want to be active and run around, having fun with friends, the way I used to, before my life changed forever. Before the accident.

I've lived alternately in two group homes and four foster families in the past three years - and none have ever come close to giving me the kind of life I used to have. The only thing I've learned to count on these past three years is the fact that you *can't* count on other people. People will tell you that they care, but they don't. They say they won't abandon you, and then they do. That's what my brother did to me.

At first, during that first year, I tried to think positively. I tried to convince myself that Tim didn't *mean* to leave me, and that he'd come back for me one day, just like he promised. But after a year had gone by, and then two, I'd changed - and so had my mindset. Tim wasn't going to come back for me. As a twelve-year-old, I'd already accepted that fact. Now, I'm thirteen - and the more time that goes by, the more I realize that I've lost all the hope I used to have, back when I was a kid. I've lost the faith I used to have in my brother and the rest of the human race.

Quietly, I go to sit down on my bed and squint at Ben's book. If I'm being honest, Ben is probably the only person that I feel I can trust at all. Although Ben is a year older than me, and the closest thing I have to an older brother in Bentwood Foster Home, I've never seen him the way I see Tim. Ben isn't overbearing or bossy. I can tell that he really cares about me, even though I know I'm hard to get along with.

Just then, Ben shuts the book and looks over at me. "Done." He stretches out his arm and offers me the book. "You sure you don't want to try it?"

I sigh and point at my bluish-green eyes. "Nah. I've got a headache."

Ben bites his lip and frowns. "When's the last time you went to the doctor?"

I rub my face with my hand and shake my head, my head hurting even more at the mere mention of doctors. "Oh, I dunno. Probably wouldn't do much good, anyways."

Ben shrugs and then stares at me for a moment. "You okay, Mark? You're quiet today."

I laugh in a bitter sort of way. "Aren't I always?"

A small smile plays across Ben's lips. "Well, sure - but not this quiet."

I roll my eyes and shake my head. "I'm fine, Ben." I hate the way Ben tries to read my thoughts - especially when he's right. Because I'm not fine. I'm tired of this life of uncertainty and waiting. I need something more.

Ben frowns at me. "I've seen that look before, Mark. Please, don't go getting any ideas. It won't do any good."

I plaster an innocent look on my face, trying to conceal the many thoughts now flying through my head. "What do you mean? What kind of ideas?"

Suddenly, a few younger boys enter the room, ending our conversation - and if the relieved look on Ben's face tells me anything, he thinks he's prevented me from 'getting any ideas.' Well, he has no clue just how many 'ideas' I've had these past three years - and now, I think I might finally have the guts to make one of them a reality.

CHAPTER THREE
TIM

The cool September wind whips through my hair as I ride my bike through the sleeping town of Greenfield, my backpack on my back and my heart beating wildly in my chest. With the number of supplies in my backpack, you'd think it would be weighing me down - but right now, I feel lighter than air, because I'm finally doing what I've wanted to do for three years.

Riding down a small hill, I slowly brake when I reach Matt's house. I coast into his backyard and hop off my bike, dragging it into the yard and laying it down gently on the grass. Suddenly, I hear the sound of a car driving past. I hurry into the backyard in order not to be seen.

Crossing my arms to stay warm in my jean jacket, I walk over to the dirty basement window that leads to Matt's bedroom. I'm about to knock on it when a voice says, "Tim?"

I whirl around to see Matt standing in front of me, completely awake with car keys in hand.

"Matt," I say, swallowing hard.

"What are you doin' here?" asks Matt, the expression on his face a mixture of confusion and amusement.

"Can't a guy go out for a little drive?" I ask, glancing at my bike and laughing casually.

Matt scoffs. "Yeah, right! You're never up at midnight. What's goin' on?"

I let the smile on my face melt, and I sigh. "Well - I was gonna tell you before, but everything happened so fast, and I just decided quickly, and I figured I shouldn't tell anybody right away so no one would know where I'm going -"

"What are you talking about?"

I bite my lip. I have to tell him. It's now or never. "I'm goin' to Charlotte, Matt."

Matt's face is full of confusion as he contemplates this. Then, suddenly, it seems to hit him. "You're biking to Charlotte. At midnight. So - I take it you don't want anyone to know where you're going?"

I shrug. "Yeah, like I said before."

Matt rubs his hand over his face and looks around the yard, as if making sure that no one else is around. Eventually, he looks at me. "Are you coming back?"

A strange feeling comes over me as I answer, "No."

"Why? I thought things were fine here. I mean, school's goin' fine. *Everything's* goin' fine."

"No, it's not," I say in a harsher tone than I mean to. I stop and take a moment to breathe.

Matt shakes his head, concern written all over his face. "What's wrong, Tim?"

I stare off into the woods that sit at the edge of Matt's backyard. I watch the way the wind makes the leaves blow, and I notice the way the colors of the leaves have already begun to change. As I'm watching all these things, I say it, all in one breath. "When my parents died, when I was fourteen, my brother and I were separated. I haven't seen him since. I'm going to Charlotte to find him."

Matt's jaw drops slightly. The first words out of his mouth - the words I was expecting to hear - are: "You have a brother?"

I nod. "Yeah."

Matt furrows his brow in thought. Then he asks, "How old is he?"

"Thirteen," I answer immediately.

"And he's in Charlotte?"

"Yeah."

Matt stares at his house for a moment, and I can almost read his thoughts. He's thinking of his little sister Sarah. He's thinking of what life would be like without her, if the two of them were separated. He's putting himself in my shoes. Then, he looks back at me and nods. "You've gotta find him."

A small smile appears on my face. "I know. You swear you won't tell anybody?"

Matt nods, his face serious. "Yeah. I swear."

He holds out his hand, and I shake it. "You don't know how much this means to me, Matt. I just had to tell somebody, and I figured you're the only person in this town who deserves a goodbye."

Matt nods and gives me a grateful smile. "Thanks, Tim. Now, you better get outta here. I wouldn't stick around much longer if I were you."

"Yeah. Bye, Matt."
  "See ya, Tim."

CHAPTER FOUR
MARK

I squint at the first page of *Ender's Game*, trying and failing to understand what the tiny words are saying - all thanks to another one of my headaches. Frustrated, I drop the book onto my bedside table with a *thud* and stare at the wall opposite from my bed. There's literally nothing to do in this place. It's so boring that it's almost got me wishing I had a new foster family - yeah, I said *almost*. Anyways, it's not really a foster family that I want. I could be on my own my whole life for all I care; it's the freedom that I want. I don't want to be anyone's responsibility. I'm tired of being tossed around and rejected by everyone I meet.

The only person in the world who might care about me is Ben, and even he shouldn't have to worry about me. I'm done with all this. I've stopped caring about finding a family. I guess I stopped years ago, but deep down I was still kind of hoping. Not anymore, though. It's time I find myself a real life instead of waiting for one that I'll never have.

I sit on my bed for a minute, letting these thoughts sink in. *A real life.* I haven't had one of those in a long time, and frankly, I don't get why I've been waiting. I'll never have the life that I used to, but maybe that's a good thing. I could have freedom and find adventure. I don't have to wait around here till I'm eighteen. I'm going to get out of here now, and never come back. I'm going to get out of Charlotte.

Footsteps and voices from down the hallway suddenly reach my ears, and my heart starts hammering. Am I really going to leave?

I turn and glance out the window that looks out into the city. I've lived in Charlotte my whole life, and not once have I ever wanted to leave. I like the fast pace of the city and the way every day has the potential to be an adventure. But when have I ever had any real adventures? If I leave now, I've got my whole life ahead of me. I'd never waste a day again. I need to leave tonight.

* * * * * * * * * *

Around 11 PM, I climb out of bed as quietly as I can and drop to the floor without a sound. I packed my backpack while everyone else was at dinner earlier tonight and hid it under my bed. Sliding it out from under the bed now, I sling it onto my back, stand up, and begin creeping towards the window.

The floor I'm on is at least 10 feet up from the ground, and the only way for me to make it outside without waking anyone up is to jump. My chances of getting hurt are…well, let's just say it's not ideal. But I've gotta do it if I want to get out of here tonight.

The window isn't locked, so I push it up to open it and stick my head out. It being late September, it's already getting a bit cooler outside. I hesitate. *Maybe I shouldn't go. Not with the weather getting cooler.* I bite my lip and almost roll my eyes at my own stupidity. *This is North Carolina. It can't get that cold. Stop making excuses.*

I look back at all the other boys who are still sound asleep. None of them will miss me, and none of them will know where I am. There really has been no better time to leave. Not even the weather can stop me now.

Swinging one leg over the side of the window ledge, I take a deep breath as I stare down at the grassy ground below. The worst that can happen is a broken bone - but that's only if I land wrong.

"One," I say quietly to myself, closing my eyes and preparing to jump. "Two."

I take one last look behind me - and that's when I spot Ben, whose eyes are wide open and locked on me.

Ben's face is almost unreadable, but there's a look in his eyes that tells me everything I need to know. He doesn't think I should go. But it's too late to go back now.

I swing my other leg over the ledge, still looking at Ben, waiting for some sort of goodbye. Finally, he raises his hand in a little wave. I return the wave and give him a little nod - and then I jump.

The fall seems slow at first, and then faster and faster, until I hit the ground with a thud that shakes me. Mud splashes up around me, and I realize I've landed in a puddle from the rain that came down from the sky earlier today.

I lay there for a minute, aching all over and wondering if anything's broken. I don't even know how I landed; it happened so fast.

I stare up and almost expect to see the sky, but all I see are patches of black, the remainder of the sky blocked by towering, shiny buildings. Part of the city is still awake, just like always.

For a split second, a pang of regret goes through me - and then I shake my head. There's not a thing in the world left for me in this city where nothing good ever seems to happen. I can't keep listening to that voice inside my head that's always telling me the opposite of what I want to hear. I have to get out of here before I make any stupid decisions - but my body hurts too much to move.

Suddenly, I can see a light turn on from a room up above and the movement of those plain, tan curtains. Then, I hear frantic voices. *They know.*

Ignoring the pain, I jump up from the wet ground and begin running, not looking back.

CHAPTER FIVE
TIM

I'm pedaling my bike down another dark, winding, nameless street when I hear a strange sound. There's a sort of 'pop' and then a 'hiss' and the next thing I know, my bike is skidding to a halt. I try pedaling harder, but this only causes the bike to begin tipping.

Instinctively, I hop off the bike and grab the handles to lay it down on the wet grass. Taking off my backpack, I reach into it and pull out a flashlight. Shining it on my bike, I peer down at the tires. What I see is exactly what I expected - the front tire has been punctured.

Feeling my heart sink in my chest, I try to pry the nail loose but to no avail.

I stand up and angrily give my bike a kick, wincing afterwards. Finally, I rub my hand over my face and sigh in defeat. I know it's no use getting angry - but after the amount of traveling I've been doing these past couple of nights, I know that I'm close to Charlotte. In fact, it pains me how close I am - because if I just had working bike tires, I know I could make it in just a couple more nights.

Standing in the darkness of this sleeping neighborhood, I weigh my options. I could stay here in whatever town

20

I'm in, and I could get a job to earn money for new bike tires. Or I could ditch my bike and find another way to travel.

I suppress the urge to groan. *Everything was going fine,* I think angrily. *So why would this happen now?*

Swallowing hard, I consider my second option. Walking on foot will take much longer. Hitchhiking is out of the question. All that's left is to stay in this town and find a job.

With this decision made, I stand up and begin dragging my bike along the street. The moon can't be seen in the sky; it's cloudy and dark, leaving me stumbling along blindly through the sleeping neighborhood, hoping that I won't run into anything.

It's only a few more minutes before I reach what I can tell is a patch of woods. How large the woods are, I don't know - but I do know that I might be able to stay there without anyone noticing me. I drag the bike into the woods, and I don't stop until there are no houses to be seen around me - just endless trees.

I continue to stumble along, waving one hand around to protect myself from unseen branches and any other obstacles ahead of me. I keep doing this until I find a large, towering tree that's settled deep in the woods. I set down my bike against the trunk and untie my sleeping bag from the back of my bike seat. I unroll it and climb in. It's not chilly, but I pull it tightly around me. Finally, I can go to sleep - but I know that I can't relax. I'm beginning to feel afraid that I can't make it all the way to Charlotte, especially with a set-back like this. Who knows how long I'll be stuck in this town?

These thoughts start to overwhelm me, and I look up, observing the leaves that are dancing in the wind. I close my eyes and let the events of the past few days sink in. I've always known that I'd find my brother - I just didn't know when. This is just a little set-back.

Finally accepting this fact, I let myself relax. All I need to worry about right now is getting the money to fix my bike - and that can wait until the morning.

* * * * * * * * * *

When I wake up the next morning, I feel well rested and optimistic. The sun is filtering through the trees, and the birds are chirping loudly. As my eyes fully adjust, I notice how large the woods really are. It's hard to believe that just a few minutes away from here is a neighborhood. I turn my gaze until I see my bike, leaning against the giant maple next to me. Ah yes, my punctured bike tire - I'm suddenly reminded of last night.

Hesitantly, I take a quick look at my watch. I wince when I see the time - it's already noon. I wanted to get up early and get a head start on looking for work, but now, half the day has been wasted.

Without another moment's hesitation, I grab my backpack, get my bearings, and begin walking quickly towards the edge of the woods. Luckily, it only takes me five minutes to reach it.

The neighborhoods don't last forever. I sense that the main part of the town is getting close, because I can hear the tell-tale sounds of cars, trucks, and busy movement. It takes only ten minutes before I reach a busy intersection, and when I turn the corner, I notice a sign for a public restroom. After a couple days on the road, I could use some washing up. Walking inside, I check to see if anyone is around. As it turns out, I'm alone.

Feeling much calmer with this knowledge, I reach into my backpack and pull out a bar of soap, a toothbrush, toothpaste, and a comb. In less than fifteen minutes, I'm washed up and ready to look for a job.

The day is hot, so I take a big chug from my newly filled thermos, trying to stay in the shade and avoid as many people as I can. Looking around, my eyes finally land on a sign that tells me where I am. I'm in the town of Davidson.

Walking through Davidson, I get hit with its small-town charm right away. The brick buildings that seem to stretch out forever are filled with smiling people. Little tables in front of beautiful restaurants are occupied with couples talking and enjoying their Saturday lunch. Murals cover the brick walls that lead into little alleyways. I take in the classic soda shop, a throwback to the 1950s, and smile at a golden retriever who walks by, leading his owner down the street.

Even as I observe all these sights, I keep my mind on the task at hand and peer into shop windows as I walk, trying to get an idea of what sort of job I should apply for. I guess that I haven't thought about it much until now. I've only ever had a job as a paperboy, but I don't think it should be too difficult to get one in some store. The hard part will be avoiding questions about my past.

My body begins to feel tired despite the amount of sleep I got last night and a loud rumble from my stomach is felt. I find some shade against a two-story brick building, find the trail mix in my backpack - and that's when I see it. A bright red sign in a large shop window with bold, white letters that read: HELP WANTED.

I hastily throw a handful of trail mix in my mouth and quickly fold the bag and put it away. Without hesitating, I stand up, walk over to the shop, and open the door to Davidson General Store for the first time.

A tall man with oversized glasses and a thin mustache is at the cash register working busily, but when the last person steps out of the check-out line, he turns his attention to me.

"Hello," he says, a warm smile on his face. "Can I help you?"

I clear my throat before I summon enough courage to say, "Um, yes, sir. I saw the sign in the window." The man looks confused, and I try to clarify. "I mean the 'help wanted' sign."

The man's face brightens. "Oh, yes! You're looking for a job?"

I nod, too nervous to trust my own tongue.

"Well, we definitely need help around here. As you can see, we're quite a large store - much larger than most of our competitors around here - and we're extremely busy every day." The man looks down at the watch on his tan wrist and smiles even more brightly. "Well, I'm on my lunch break now, but I'm eager to get to know you, son. What do you say we get you in for an interview, eh?"

I raise my eyebrows. "R - really? Right now?"

"Sure." He tilts his head and looks at me over his spectacles, which magically stay on the tip of his sharp nose. "Well, there's no time like the present, right?" I take a deep breath, smile, and nod. The man looks over his shoulder and yells, "Stanley, watch the register for me, will you?"

With that, the two of us walk behind the check-out line to a door that leads to a tidy, but small space of an office.

The man nods at a chair beside a wooden desk. "Have a seat," he says, and I do, suddenly realizing how much my feet hurt, and how good it feels to relax in an actual chair, and not on a bike or the grass.

The man sits down in his executive chair on the other side of the desk, and he leans forward. "Let's start with introductions. My name is Jack Kilmer, and I am the owner of this establishment."

"It's nice to meet you, Mr. Kilmer," I say hesitantly, self-consciously running a hand through my light brown hair. "I'm Tim Ryder."

"Nice to meet you, Tim," says Mr. Kilmer with a grin. "So, you're looking for a job?"

"Yes, sir."

"And how old are you, Tim?" asks Mr. Kilmer.

"Seventeen," I answer.

"Do you have any experience?"

I nod. "Yeah, um, I held up a paper route where I used to live. Haven't worked in a store before, but I'll do anything you need doing. I'm a quick-learner and I'm free every day!"

Mr. Kilmer crosses his arms and leans forward. "What about school?" I feel the eager look disappear from my face. School? I never thought about school. I should have known that people would ask questions. I want to tell the truth - but I can't. Not when I'm so close to getting the job.

"Oh, well, after school, of course," I say, trying to sound sure of myself. Thankfully, Mr. Kilmer nods.

I almost breathe a sigh of relief; I have a feeling that Mr. Kilmer isn't the kind of man to pry too much into things like school. After a short moment of silence, he says, "Okay, Tim. I'm going to hire you as a cashier. You'll work weekdays, and you'll earn four dollars an hour."

I feel my jaw drop open slightly. I wonder if I'm asleep. The man must be joking. *Four dollars an hour.* That's more than I made on my paper route. I won't have to stay in the town for as long as I thought.

"Yes, sir. I'll take it."

Mr. Kilmer smiles. "When can you start?"

CHAPTER SIX
MARK

It's a strange feeling, not knowing where I am.

For the past two days, I've been traveling through dense woods, taking my time, and sleeping as much as I want, so I can keep my strength up. I'm in no hurry. Now that I'm a safe distance away from the foster home, I have this sense of freedom that I've never felt before. I can do whatever I want whenever I want, and no one's around to tell me what to do. Even though my focus right now is traveling, and reaching *some* destination far away from Charlotte, I know that one day soon, I'll be able to live the kind of life I've wanted for so long.

Now, however, I'm not quite sure where I am. I don't have a map or a compass; I've simply been walking in one direction, knowing that the further I walk, the further I am from Charlotte, and my old life.

I've never really been in the woods before. My family never went camping or fishing. We never really left the city. We just kept on living that tiring, meaningless existence in that hectic, clamorous town. The odd thing was that no one seemed to care much - except for me. I always knew that I wanted to get out of the city and find some real adventure. Now, that's happening - and I wish it had happened sooner.

27

Mostly, I've been looking around the dry, bright green woods, fascinated by all the unfamiliar sights and sounds - but today, rain is pattering on the tall trees that surround me, and the air is wet and cool. Thankfully, the canopy of leaves above my head keeps me mostly dry.

I'm slowly becoming used to the sounds of the woods, such as sticks crunching underneath my feet or the owl that kept me awake most of last night. At first, I found myself almost jumping at sounds like these, too used to the sounds of cars honking instead. Now, I'm enjoying these sounds - because to me, they're a sign that my past is behind me.

Suddenly, the wind seems to pick up a bit. I cross my arms and shiver as the cold rain comes down harder, penetrating the leafy umbrella above. I'm wearing a jacket and jeans, but they aren't protecting me from the cold rain. I hold out my skinny, pale hands and cup them together. They don't gather much rain, but I take the small amount and pour as much as I can into my mouth, immediately losing the parched feeling I've had all day. There's no point in letting all that water gather on my head instead of in my mouth.

I continue trudging on with my arms crossed, not bothering to avoid the muddy puddles that have begun to form on the damp, green ground. That's when I hear it - the sound of footsteps coming from behind me.

I stop walking suddenly. As soon as I do, the other footsteps halt, as well. Without hesitation, I spin around and find myself staring at a little boy who's standing just about six feet behind me.

At first, I don't say anything. I only observe the boy curiously. He looks to be about seven years old, judging by his small stature and innocent, freckled face. His wet hair is bright red - redder than any hair I've seen before. His eyes are a bright, vivid green, and filled with a sort of depth that I notice immediately.

Taking all this in, I clear my throat and say, "Who are you?"

The boy merely blinks at me and stuffs his hands in his pockets, obviously cold.

I try again. "What's your name?"

Still no answer.

Beginning to become frustrated, I sigh, turn around, and continue walking. The sound of the boy's footsteps resumes as well. Ignoring this, I walk without looking back, focused on keeping my head down to avoid the rain. After a few minutes, however, my curiosity gets the better of me, and I turn around again. The boy stops walking and simply stares at me.

I sigh again, trying to show how annoyed I am. "*Why* are you following me?"

The boy doesn't answer.

Fed up, I shake my head and groan. "Come on, what's your name?"

The boy takes a few steps closer to me and looks me over for a moment. Finally, his mouth opens, and in a tiny voice, he says, "Josh."

I blink in surprise. "Josh. Okay. Uh, hi."

Josh nods in reply. Then, to my astonishment, he asks, "What's your name?"

I raise my eyebrows. I guess it's only fair that he should ask me that question. "Mark," I answer. Venturing further, I ask, "How old are you?"

"Seven. How old are you?"

"Thirteen." The two of us stand in silence for a few seconds, watching each other in suspense, wondering what the other is going to do next.

Eventually, I can't stand to wait any longer. "What are you doing out here?" I ask.

For a moment, Josh doesn't reply. Then, standing tall, he says boldly, "What are *you* doing out here?"

Knowing that I've been beaten, I answer the little boy without hesitation. "Traveling."

"Where?"

I laugh almost bitterly. "As far away from Charlotte as I can get."

Josh cocks his head in thought. "You want to get away from Charlotte?"

"Yes."

To my surprise, Josh smiles. "So do I."

* * * * * * * * * *

"So, what are you doing out here?" I ask.

Josh and I have been walking for a little while, waiting for the rain to slow down. Now that it's only drizzling and the sun is shining, we're sitting across from each other, resting. My goal is to finally get some information out of the boy and find out why he's following me - but so far, he's been quiet.

I watch as he contemplates answering my question. His green eyes seem to carry many thoughts behind them - thoughts that I doubt he's going to reveal anytime soon.

"Well - you promise you won't tell anyone?"

I shrug, thinking to myself, *There isn't anyone around here to tell.* "I promise."

Josh bites his lip before saying, "I - I ran away."

I nod. I suspected as much. "Where from?"

"A foster home."

"Which one?"

"Willowview."

I can feel my eyebrows shoot up on my forehead. "Willowview? But - well, I used to live there!"

Josh's eyes widen. "You did? How long ago?"

"A couple years."

"Oh. Well, I got transferred there about a year ago. I guess we never would have seen each other."

I nod. Then, I ask, "Why'd you run away?"

Josh looks away suddenly and shakes his head. I know then that he doesn't plan on revealing everything to me at once. I frown but don't push him any further.

Looking around, I observe the way the sun is casting a beautiful golden glow on the woods. The rain has stopped completely, except for the few leftover drops that are slipping off of the bright green leaves.

"Well," I say suddenly, standing up, "I'd better be going."

Josh leaps to his feet, his eyes wide. "But - but you can't. I mean, you just sat down."

"Yeah, I know. Can't stop long, though. Gotta keep on moving."

Josh darts in front of me, and I notice a desperate look in his green eyes that wasn't there before. "Please?" he says. "Can't I travel with you?"

My jaw drops open slightly. Of all the things that Josh might've said, that was the one I was least expecting. "You? Travel with me?"

Josh nods earnestly. "Yes. I promise I'll be good. I'll listen to everything you say - I promise. Please, Mark?"

I take a moment to think about this. Josh is only seven years old, and he's all alone - the best thing I could do for him would be to let him stay with me. On the other hand, he's too young to be able to handle the life that I'm looking for - a life of adventure. I'm not capable of taking care of a little kid. I've never been good with kids, and I've never had the experience of being an older brother. But still, I can't just leave him here.

With a sigh of resolve, I nod slowly. "Sure. You can stay with me."

Immediately, Josh's big eyes crinkle from smiling, and from that reaction, I know I've done the right thing - I hope.

CHAPTER SEVEN
TIM

I work busily, a smile plastered on my face. Today is my first day working at the grocery store, and while it's been hours since I started, I'm still nervous. I know this because I've wiped my sweaty palms on my blue plaid shirt more than once. But despite this, I'm doing as well as I hoped I would. I'm relieved to see that Mr. Kilmer seems to think so, too.

He watched me closely all morning, but now, a few minutes away from five o'clock, he barely glances over in my direction. I guess he already trusts me to do a good job - or maybe he's just too preoccupied with customers to worry about me. Either way, things are going well.

All day, I've been watching Mr. Kilmer out of the corner of my eye, trying to do everything that he does. He always seems to be smiling, since there's a steady line of customers at his check-out line, so I've been smiling, too. He works fast but talks clearly, so I try to do that, too. I'm guessing that Mr. Kilmer has been working here for a long time; it's obvious that he knows what he's doing. I wonder how long it would take me to become as professional and skilled as him. It's not as if I'll ever accomplish this, though - I'll be out of here in a couple weeks at the most.

I quickly glance up at the clock on the wall. It's a minute away from five o'clock now, but I still have a couple customers in line.

Soon, the last person reaches me, a tall, middle-aged woman with short, blonde hair, and I greet her with the same smile that I've worn all day. "Hello, ma'am. Did you find everything okay?" I say, trying to muster up enough energy not to sound as tired as I am.

The woman smiles at me and nods. "Yes, thank you." I bag her groceries quickly, and she hands me exact cash with a look of self-importance.

As soon as she walks out of the store, I look over at Mr. Kilmer, waiting for him to give me some sort of signal. Right away, he makes eye contact with me and gives me a wave. "Good job today, Tim. See you tomorrow."

I grin. "Thank you, sir. See you then." Taking off my white apron and laying it down on my side of the checkout counter, I run my fingers through my hair as I walk out the door and into the fresh, September air.

Walking briskly down Main Street, I turn the corner too quickly. The next thing I know, I end up on the ground next to a dazed-looking girl with the most dazzling green eyes I've ever seen.

"Oh!" I exclaim, my cheeks flushing. "I'm - I'm so sorry -"

"That's okay," replies the girl, laughing sheepishly.

I immediately extend my hand to help the girl up, and she takes it, standing and dusting off her green sweatshirt and acid-washed jeans.

I take this moment to observe the girl. As soon as I get a good look at her, my heart catches in my chest. The most beautiful girl I've ever seen is standing in front of me - and I just bowled her over, just because I was in such a hurry.

The girl's eyes are one of her most beautiful features - but then, there's her hair. Her long, wavy, strawberry-blonde hair that flows over her shoulders. I find myself staring at it in a sort of daze.

"So, you must be in a big hurry, huh?" laughs the girl, looking up at me.

I blink and gulp. The sound of that laugh... I can't get enough of it. I want to hear it again. And then, there's that smile - it's pearly white, and makes me want to smile, too.

"Uh, yeah - yeah," I stammer. "I really am sorry. I should've been looking where I was going. I was just - excited, that's all."

"About what?" smiles the girl.

I bite my lip. "Oh, uh, new job. Nothing to get that distracted over, though."

The girl tilts her head and stares at me, still smiling. "What's your name? I've never seen you around here before."

"Tim Ryder. What's yours?"

"Kate Woodland."

Kate Woodland. I want to repeat that name on my lips - so I do.

"Nice to meet you, Kate Woodland," I smile, holding out my hand. She shakes it and grins.

"So, have you lived around here long?"

I shake my head. "Nope. My family just moved in a couple days ago."

"Oh, what neighborhood?"

"Uhh -" I scratch my head. "Can't seem to remember. I don't have the address memorized yet - haven't really had time, you know."

"Oh, sure," nods Kate. Suddenly, she takes a glance at her watch, grimaces, and looks back up at me. "I've gotta go, but I'll see you around. It was nice to meet you, Tim!"

"You, too, Kate." I watch as she jogs down the street, her long hair flying behind her. Just like that, from one conversation, this much is clear: I *have* to get to know Kate Woodland.

* * * * * * * * * *

I've been walking aimlessly for about a half an hour now, unable to think about anything or anyone but Kate Woodland. I come upon a sparkling, blue lake. There are no people around, and the sound of water splashing softly lures me to the dock. I walk onto it and sit down on the edge, my hands clasped together.

I've never been this enamored by a girl before - especially not from a first meeting. But somehow, I can't get the image of her smiling face out of my head. I can't stop thinking about her eyes, her dimples, and her laugh. And her beautiful, melodic voice.

I feel my heart thumping in my chest, and I take a few deep breaths to slow it down. I can't get crazy about a girl right now; in fact, this is probably the worst timing for that to happen. But for some reason, I feel as if I have no control over the situation. All I want right now is to get to know Kate Woodland.

Frustrated at my own inability to control myself, I stare out at the water and try to think of something - *anything* - to distract me. So, I start to think about my brother.

Mark was always energetic and full of life. Even when he was tired, you'd never know it. He was always willing to talk someone's ear off and become their friend - but he was also willing to get into trouble. In fact, it happened more times than I can count, and always over the silliest things. The only time that I can remember when it *wasn't* silly was when I was involved.

Mark and I had been outside, playing basketball in an alleyway with a few friends. Everything was going fine, and we were all having a good time. I was initially surprised by this, since all the boys were my twelve-year-old friends, and Mark was a whole four years younger than us - but he held his own and proved that he was a decent basketball player.

We'd almost finished the game when my friend Rod decided to pull a cheap trick on the other team. He pushed our friend Chris onto the ground - with too much force, I should add. This angered Chris immediately.

"What do you think you're doing, Harrison?" he exclaimed. "You think that's funny?"

"Well, you're just a little too tall to play with us, Chris," replied Rod with a smirk. "Had to push you down so you weren't towering over me like a giant."

Chris, whose height was a sore subject, stalked towards Rod, his cheeks flaming. "Yeah? Well, how do you like this?"

Chris threw his fist towards Rod, but by stupid instinct, Mark leapt towards them in time to stop him. "Don't hurt him, Chris," he exclaimed.

I opened my mouth to say something, but nothing came out. I guess I figured Chris would cool down and take it easy - but he didn't.

Shoving Mark onto the ground, he spit out, "Who asked you, Ryder? You're pathetic - you and your big brother. Got that from your daddy, didn't you, boy?"

I ran towards Chris in a sudden fit of anger, ramming him into a wall much harder than I anticipated. Still, I didn't back down. "Get outta here, Baker. You got that?" I sneered, grabbing at his shirt collar.

Chris tore away from my grasp, his eyes narrowed. "Yeah. I got it."

I watched as he went stalking down the alleyway and turned the corner. Then I turned back to the rest of the boys, who were watching me with a strange mix of terror and admiration on their faces. I didn't want their admiration - all I wanted was to be alone. "See you, guys," I said quietly.

No one hesitated to leave. Rod picked up his basketball and walked over to me. "Hey, I'm sorry, Tim. I didn't know he'd get so upset."

I shook my head, avoiding eye contact. "Forget it. It's over."

Rod shrugged and walked away, regret in his eyes. I took a deep breath and looked down at my hands. They were shaking, and I couldn't seem to make them stop.

I turned and looked at Mark, laying a hand on his bony shoulder. He was looking at me with admiration, too - but there was something else in his expression which I could read immediately. I knew what it was because I was feeling it, too. Our family had been insulted - and we both wondered how much truth was in his words.

That day, a sort of unspoken promise was made between us. It was a promise to always defend each other and our family name, no matter how tainted it may or may not be.

I stare at the flaming orange sun setting over the sparkling blue water, and I wonder if I've already broken that promise.

CHAPTER EIGHT
TIM

Today is Friday and the end of my first week at work - which also means it's payday. For this reason, I've found myself distracted all day. The prospect of receiving my first week's pay has me more excited than I ever thought I would be about money. That isn't the only reason I'm distracted, though. I'm distracted because I know that at any moment, Kate Woodland could walk into the store and give me the chance to hear that beautiful laugh and look into those deep, green eyes.

I'm just bagging the groceries of a smiling, elderly couple when it happens. I glance over at the door and see Kate walking inside. At that moment, she looks over at me - and we make eye contact.

In a panic, I stand up straight and accidentally knock over the bottle of milk I was about to put in the paper bag. Apparently, it wasn't sealed correctly, because its contents begin leaking and spreading across the checkout counter - right as Kate begins walking towards me.

"Oh, no," I groan, standing the bottle upright and grabbing some paper towels that I have lying under the counter. "I'm really sorry, I -"

"It's alright," says the woman, adjusting her glasses and giving me a sympathetic look that leads me to believe she knows the cause of my clumsiness.

"Let me get a new one," I stammer, moving to leave the counter and retrieve a bottle.

"No, no, don't worry about it. I'll get one," says the man, giving me a comforting smile and leaving.

A moment later, he returns with another bottle, and I almost breathe a sigh of relief. Still, I can't feel relaxed knowing that Kate is standing nearby, watching the whole embarrassing scene.

I try to smile as I finish ringing up the couple's groceries. When I finish and say goodbye, I busy myself with wiping up the last few drops of milk on the counter and try not to look up - even when I can sense Kate's presence moving closer to me.

"Hey," I hear her say in that melodic voice of hers.

Gulping, I straighten up and look her right in the eye. "H - hi. Kate, right?"

Kate grins. "Yeah. And you're Tim."

I smile. "Yep." Suddenly, I feel the need to explain my current, frazzled state. "You kind of caught me at a bad time. Well - I had a bit of a mess-up."

Kate's smile disappears immediately. "Oh - I'm sorry. Should I go? I don't want to distract you from your job or anything."

"No, no, it's totally fine!" I exclaim a little too eagerly as I glance up at the clock on the wall. "I'm on my break now. Are you here to shop?"

Nodding, Kate's smile returns, causing my heart to beat faster. "Yeah, I told my parents I'd pick up a few things, but it can totally wait if you want company on your break."

* * * * * * * * * *

"We moved here when I was four. Both my parents went to college here, and I guess they missed it so much that they came back."

"Wow," I say. "You've been here a long time, then."

"Yeah. Almost my whole life. I guess you could say I know this town like the back of my hand. I know all the people, too. Well - except you," says Kate, who has barely taken a breath for the past ten minutes.

As if to prove this fact, Kate looks to the right, where Mr. Kilmer has just walked over to his checkout counter, and waves. "Hello, Mr. Kilmer."

"Well, hi, Kate," replies Mr. Kilmer. "How are you today? I see you've met my newest employee."

"Yes, I have." Kate looks at me, and I avert my gaze, acutely aware that I'm blushing.

A knowing look passes over Mr. Kilmer's face, and he nods slowly. "Well, I'll let you two visit. Carry on," he says, turning to the customers who've just stepped into his line.

Gratefully, I smile at him before turning back to Kate. "So. What do you like to do around here?"

Kate twirls a strand of strawberry-blonde hair as she thinks for a moment. "Hm. Well, I love kayaking on Lake Norman. Have you gotten to see it yet?"

I remember the lake I stopped at earlier in the week, and I nod. "Yeah. Kayaking sounds fun. What else?"

"Oh, shopping, bike riding. I like watching the college's basketball games, too."

I raise my eyebrows. "You like basketball?"

"Yeah, I love it. Do you?"

A thousand childhood memories race through my mind as I think about that one sport that I played continuously as a kid in Charlotte. Slowly, I nod. "Yes."

Suddenly, I feel a pain in my stomach, and I wince.

"Are you okay?" asks Kate, a concerned look on her face.

"Oh, yeah, just hungry. Hey, speaking of which, do you know of any good restaurants around here?"

Kate nods excitedly. "Yes. Red's Diner is the best place around. It's just down the street and probably my favorite restaurant. It's got the best hamburgers; you should try it sometime."

On impulse, I meet Kate's eyes, and without hesitating, I ask, "Would you like to meet up there sometime? To hang out?"

I don't have to wait even half a second. Kate is nodding the moment I finish talking. "Yes," she grins. "How about tomorrow? Does six o'clock sound good?"

I breathe a sigh of relief. "Sounds great."

* * * * * * * * * *

At five o'clock, Mr. Kilmer approaches me with a wad of cash in his hand. Trying not to appear too eager, I hesitate before taking it.

"You've done a good job this week, Tim. You deserve this," says Mr. Kilmer. "I'm still waiting on a few bits of info like your social security number - oh, it's no bother, I understand what it's like to not find all your stuff after a move. I'll just be paying you in cash for now."

I smile. "Thank you, sir. Have a nice day." Taking off my apron and throwing on my backpack, I rush out of the store, a hop in my step. I don't stop until I've reached the YMCA. Leaning against the side of the building, I finally take a moment to look through my pay, counting it up and feeling a sense of freedom and independence.

Without waiting a second more, I rush inside the YMCA. Ten minutes later, I've rented a room.

After a long, hot shower and a fresh change of clothes courtesy of the washer and dryer down the hall, I sigh contentedly. For the first time in a long while, I feel as if I have some control over my own life.

In fact, I'm so happy - and hungry - that I decide to venture over to Red's Diner to try one of those hamburgers that Kate told me about.

With this thought in mind, I turn around and walk deeper into the town. I see small, charming clothing stores, a pharmacy with candy in the window, and some 'mom and pop' restaurants - but it's the last of these that draws my attention. As my stomach growls, I walk a little faster towards the restaurant that I see a few doors down.

The second I walk inside Red's Diner, I feel a sense of calm. This place has a cozy, homey feeling, with a jukebox sitting in the corner.

I hear the song "Uptown Girl" by Billy Joel begin to play, and I remember hearing that song for the first time at my spring school dance in 1983 - right before everything in my life changed.

"Can I help you? Hello?"

I come back to reality and order a cheeseburger, fries, and a 7UP.

"I'll take one of these, too, thanks," I say as I grab a newspaper from the pile on the counter.

Cozy in my booth, I peruse the paper. After checking out the front-page headlines and the sports section, I flip to the arts and entertainment. The first article is about a new musical that's opening in London called *The Phantom of the Opera*. The second is about the success of the new movie starring Tom Cruise, called *Top Gun*. I remember seeing the movie in the theater with Matt; we watched every scene in fascination, amazed at the fighter jets and enjoying the music. After glancing over the second article, I turn the page and immediately see a picture of a smiling little boy - a missing child. Name: Joshua O'Brien. Age: Seven. Hair Color: Red.

He's so young to be all alone, I think to myself. This steers my thoughts towards my brother, giving me a renewed sense of urgency. I know I have to find him as soon as I can; he doesn't deserve to wait any longer for me than he already has.

Then, in the back of my mind, a name repeats itself over and over again: *Kate*. I'm already scheduled to meet with her at the diner tomorrow. I've never had the nerve to ask a girl out so suddenly before. I can't let her down so soon.

I think for a moment before coming to a decision. I'll meet with Kate tomorrow and just get to know her a little bit. Then, on Monday, I'll buy a new tire and head out to find my brother.

CHAPTER NINE
MARK

"Hey kid, let's stop for a little while."

I glance down at the skinny, red-haired little boy who's been walking silently beside me for the past two days. His eyes are partly closed, signaling to me that it's time to rest. The last thing I want to do is tire Josh out, especially while I know that he probably has eaten very little in a few days. Looking up at the sky, I realize that it's getting lighter quickly. For the past few hours, we've traveled on the side of a dusty road, knowing that we won't be seen in the dark - but I know it's time to move back into the woods.

"What?" mumbles Josh, taking a moment to open his eyes wider. I take his pale, freckled arm and lead him towards the woods, where the two of us sit down under the shade of a tall oak tree.

I watch as Josh sits down slowly, a look of pain and exhaustion in his eyes, and I decide that now is a good time to split the last granola bar that I packed. I pull out the granola bar, split it, and offer one half to Josh.

Immediately, Josh's green eyes light up, but he shakes his head. "I'm okay," he says, his voice barely above a whisper. "I've done just fine so far, haven't I?"

I blink in surprise. "Well, sure you have - but you've gotta eat, don't you? Come on, it's okay. It's the last one I've got, but I figure we should eat it now before we get too hungry."

Hesitantly, Josh reaches out and accepts his half. He chews and swallows it in about five seconds. Smiling in spite of myself, I refuse to eat that quickly. I don't want Josh to think I'm that hungry. In fact, *I* don't want to think I'm that hungry. I need to keep my strength up if I'm going to get Josh and I to a safe place.

As if he's reading my thoughts, Josh looks up at me and asks, "What will we do next? To find food, I mean."

I swallow my half of the granola bar hard. "Uh - well, I figured we'd just find some town to crash in and stay there for a while. We can always pick up and keep moving, but I think we've traveled pretty far, don't you?"

Josh nods slowly, contemplating this. "Yes - if you don't think we'll get caught. You don't think that - do you?"

I shake my head firmly, trying to act more confident than I am. "No, of course I don't think that. It's easy to get lost. Don't worry, no one's gonna find us."

Josh bites his lip and turns his head to stare at the rays of sun being cast throughout the woods. To anyone else, the look on Josh's face may be unreadable - but I understand it perfectly. I understand it better than anyone, because I know I've worn it on my face before. It's the look of a boy who is so unsure of the world that even a promise made by the friendliest person couldn't reassure him.

I'm about to look away and let Josh be alone with his thoughts - but I halt when I notice his big, green eyes begin to water. Just like that, I feel an imaginary knife cut through my heart.

I'd almost forgotten what it was like to feel sad for someone else. Life's been so rough on me that I guess I became too well-acquainted with my own sadness. And now, here I am, faced with someone else's pain, and I don't know how to deal with it. To top it off, I especially don't know how to deal with the pain of a seven-year-old boy.

I watch Josh out of the corner of my eye. He looks so lost and alone, as if his mind is in a thousand places at once. All I want to do right now is rescue him and tell him that everything is going to be okay.

"H - hey," I stammer, trying to sound soothing and reassuring. "Everything's gonna be fine. I promise. No one's gonna find us - and even if they did, I wouldn't let anything happen to you, alright?" Awkwardly, I place a hand on his shoulder and give it a pat.

Josh rubs his eyes before looking up at me and giving a smile. "Okay."

* * * * * * * * * *

I've never felt like such a hypocrite before.

I don't know what I'm doing. I don't know where Josh and I are, and I don't know how we're going to make it another day without food. Most of all, I don't know how to be a big brother - and yet, here I am, traveling with a seven-year-old boy who probably needs much more than a 'brother figure' can give him.

What he needs, a voice whispers in my mind, *are parents.*

Immediately, I feel as if I've been punched in the gut. Josh doesn't need parents - and neither do I. I've gotten along just fine so far, and so has he. It isn't our fault that we don't have what everyone else seems to have. It isn't our fault that we're on our own. That's just what we were handed in life, and we're dealing with it as well as anyone else could.

As for being a brother, I think I can handle that just fine. It can't be that hard, really. Most older brothers just offer protection, advice, and the advantage of being stronger. I can do all those things. After all, Tim did it, so why can't I?

I swallow hard as I think of Tim. He was a good older brother - and he was different. He wasn't like my friends' brothers. While they tried to spend as much time away from their younger brothers as possible, Tim never really minded when I joined in on a basketball game with his friends. He spent time with me; he helped me with my homework in the middle of the night, taught me how to handle bullies, and gave me a point of view in life that my parents couldn't share with me. He was my older brother, and I looked up to him.

I wasn't aware of how different he was from other people's brothers until one day when my friend Alex and I were playing catch by his apartment. It wasn't a long walk from my family's apartment, so when dinnertime rolled around, Tim walked over to bring me back home.

"Hey, Mark, we've gotta go," he said, after greeting Alex.

Immediately, I folded my arms and frowned. "But I just got out here a half hour ago. That's not long enough."

Tim shook his head, a thirteen-year-old look of authority on his face. "Well, Ma said dinner's ready now. You don't wanna keep her waiting, Mark."

I frowned even harder and stayed planted on the sidewalk. "Not *yet*."

Tim gave me a look that I could read easily. It read, *Mom has enough on her plate. Come home now.*

I should have been understanding. I should have listened to him - but I didn't. "Give me half an hour, Tim. Just half an hour. I promise I'll come home then. You know Ma'll understand."

But Tim *didn't* know that. I didn't know it, either. Still, all I cared about was being away from home a little while longer.

Eventually, Tim let out a sigh and nodded slowly. "Okay. Fine. Go ahead - but not any more than half an hour, Mark. She needs us at home."

I grinned. "I got it. Thanks, Tim."

Tim gave me a small smile but sighed again in spite of this. As he walked away, Alex stared at me, his eyes bulging. "Man, your brother's rad. My brother would never let me get away with something like that - he'd just pick me up and carry me home."

I nodded and began thinking about this. Finally, I understood: My brother was different. He let me get away with things sometimes. He liked me, even if I was four years younger. He cared about me. I smiled as I realized, *I'm proud of my brother*.

Now, I wonder how I could be such an idiot.

* * * * * * * * * *

"Mark? Are you awake?" a small voice asks.

Rubbing my face with my hand, I blink a few times and let my eyes adjust to my surroundings. It's dark now with a few traces of sunlight left, and I can tell the sun has just set. Sitting up, I find myself face-to-face with Josh, who has obviously been awake just a little longer than me, given his mussed red hair and sleepy green eyes.

"Yeah, yeah, I'm awake." I sit up all the way and continue rubbing my face, taking my time to wake up.

"Well, when should we start moving? The sun just set, so if my calculations are correct, we should have about fourteen hours to travel in the dark."

My eyes widen in surprise as I look at Josh, who's speaking as if he's many years older than he is. "Um - yeah, we can walk now." I stand up, and the two of us begin walking.

At first, we walk in silence, but my curiosity quickly gets the better of me. "So - did you always live in Charlotte?" I ask, stepping over a small log.

Josh hops over the log with ease and shrugs. "Yeah. I mean - I think so."

We continue walking for a few minutes as my mind races for something else to say. Eventually, we exit the woods and find ourselves walking on a back road again. Thankfully, only the occasional car seems to pass by, due to the fact that it's nighttime.

I clear my throat before asking, "Ever been to any other places? Like, on trips or something?"

Josh shakes his head. He stares straight ahead, refusing to make eye contact with me. "No. I was young when I was left at Crosspoint. That's the first foster home I ever lived in."

I nod. "So you were there for a long time, then?"

Josh thinks for a moment. "Yes. That is, when I wasn't with different foster families."

I nod again. "Oh." At the mere mention of foster families, my thoughts go spiraling as I remember all the homes I've lived in the past three years. I was always advised to go to great lengths to 'impress' the families and to 'be good,' but the way I always saw it was, why should I be the one trying to impress them? Shouldn't it be the other way around?

My thoughts are interrupted when I notice Josh staring at me curiously. "What is it?" I ask, suddenly feeling nervous.

"When were you left at your foster home, Mark?" asks Josh.

I swallow hard and open my mouth to reply, but no words come out. I wasn't expecting Josh to ask me about my past. I guess I should have.

"Three years ago."

Josh cocks his head and continues to look at me, as if trying to read my thoughts. "Oh. Did your parents leave you?"

At first, I only feel confused. "What? No," I say, almost defensively. Then, I realize where Josh must be coming from, and I feel sick to my stomach. "I mean - no," I say, calmer this time. "They… died. In a car accident."

The curious look on Josh's face immediately melts into one of pity. I look away quickly; I hate it when people look at me like that.

Then, suddenly, Josh steps forward and wraps his skinny arms around me in a hug. "I'm sorry," he says in a muffled voice.

I force a smile. "Thanks," I say, patting him on the back. This almost makes me feel better - but it doesn't. Because all I can think is, *I should be the one saying 'sorry' to him.*

CHAPTER TEN
MARK

I turn around and realize that Josh has fallen behind me a few steps. Waiting for him to catch up to me, I notice the way his face has become paler than before, and how his lips appear dry and cracked. I take a deep breath as I come to the only conclusion I can: We need to find shelter, food, and water, and *fast*.

"Josh," I say, thinking as I talk, "let's take our time. We'll keep walking a little while, until we find a place to stay. I promise, the first safe place we see, we'll crash there, and we can stay there as long as we can."

A small smile appears on Josh's face as he nods. "Alright."

The two of us begin walking again - although this time, I slow my pace in order not to rush the little boy. We walk in silence for a little while, the wind whistling softly in my ears. It hasn't rained all night, but the ground is soft beneath my feet, still a bit damp from yesterday.

Suddenly, before I know what's happening, I see a tiny speck in the distance. A speck that resembles a building. I begin running ahead, going faster than my legs can carry me.

"Mark!" yells Josh. "Where are you going?"

"There's a house!" I reply, shouting over my shoulder. "I can see it, just ahead!"

Letting out a gasp, Josh immediately goes running after me, his feet flying. As I run, I can see the sun beginning to rise. My first instinct is to look around and make sure that no one's around to see Josh and I - but I don't need to look. We've traveled into the woods, and simply from the fact that I can't hear any cars or busy towns, I know that we're a safe distance away from civilization.

Eventually, I stop running - and so does Josh. Because right in front of us is a small, rustic cabin.

It takes a moment for me to realize that Josh is calling my name. "Mark? Mark? What are you doing?"

I don't reply. My brain is working faster than my body can keep up with, and I begin pacing in front of the cabin, examining the windows and peering inside. I see no cars parked outside and no sign of people inside giving me hope that this is a summer cottage whose owners will not return for some time.

"Mark," says Josh, "are you thinking about going in there?"

I stop and turn around, nodding. "Why not?"

Josh watches as I walk over to the front door and reach out to open it. Holding my breath in anticipation, I turn the doorknob. As I suspected, the door is locked.

I suppress the urge to groan as I look at Josh. His face has fallen, and he looks even smaller and tired than before. I can't give up on him now. If we could have gotten in the house, it would have been a perfect place for us to stay. The wheels in my brain begin turning as an idea pops into my head. I crouch down in front of the house.

The little boy stares at me in confusion. "Mark? What are you doing?"

Without replying, I begin turning up the rocks that sit around the front of the house. Finding the biggest one, I roll it over - and find a key sitting underneath. My heart leaps in excitement as I stand up and turn the key inside the doorknob. The door swings open easily, and Josh steps inside. Immediately, his eyes look as if they're going to pop out of his head. "Mark! Come in here and look at this!"

Too excited to speak, I take one step inside the cabin. The next thing I know, I'm standing in the middle of a warm living room, completely furnished with the coziest-looking couch, loveseat, and armchair. A coffee table sits in the middle of the rest of the furniture. Josh doesn't hesitate to rush forward and collapse onto the couch, a large grin on his freckled face. "Ohh," he sighs. "It's so comfortable. Sit down, Mark."

Hesitantly, I slowly cross through the room and gently sit down on the couch. "Yeah," I agree. "It's nice."

I haven't been sitting for more than five seconds when Josh hops up again with newfound energy. "Let's look at the rest of the place!"

Following Josh, we explore the cabin for the next few minutes or so, going in and out of each room cautiously. Then, finally, we come to the kitchen. I hold my breath as I approach one of the cabinets. *Here it is,* I think to myself. *The moment of truth.*

To my utter surprise, I open the cabinet to be faced with my number one wish: Food. Too excited to speak, I whirl around and simply grin at Josh. He's facing me with the same sort of shocked smile. "Well - let's eat something. I'm hungry," he says.

I laugh for the first time in a while, overjoyed beyond belief. Josh and I have now found two furnished bedrooms, a bathroom with running water, a living room, and - most importantly - a modestly stocked kitchen. The fridge is mostly empty except for some ketchup and hot sauce, but the pantry has oatmeal, cereal, and canned fruits and vegetables.

Without waiting another minute, I eagerly open a can of pears and grab two glasses from the cabinet. I fill up both glasses with water and then carry them with the can of pears and two forks out to the living room, where Josh and I sit down on the couch, right across from a large painting of a lake hanging on the wall. As we eat, I marvel at our luck - and wonder how long it's going to last.

Still, Josh and I are tired, and we can't keep traveling if we don't let ourselves rest a while. After a few minutes of sitting on the couch, I glance over my shoulder down the hallway, and then back at Josh. "What do you say we get some sleep now?"

Josh, whose mouth is full, simply nods. The two of us stand up, leaving the forks and empty cans on the coffee table, and we head over to the hallway. I step into one bedroom, and Josh walks into the other.

Standing in my new room, overwhelmed by the peace and silence of the cabin, I walk over to the window and stare out at the woods. The sun has almost completely risen now, but I've become used to sleeping during the day.

Feeling my eyelids become heavy, I'm just about to sit down on the bed and fall asleep when Josh walks in the room.

Thinking out loud, I say, "I've never had my own room before."

Josh blinks. "Oh. Really?"

I nod.

"Where did you used to live? I mean when you were younger."

I kick back and lay down, closing my eyes and getting ready to fall asleep. "An apartment. My brother and I shared a room."

"You have a brother?" asks Josh in surprise.

I open my eyes, suddenly regretting that I said anything. I hate talking about Tim - so I don't understand how those words slipped so easily out of my mouth.

"Yeah," is all I say.

Josh cocks his head in thought. "How old is he?"

"Seventeen."

"What was it like?"

"What was *what* like?"

"Having a brother?"

60

I swallow hard and try to act casual. "Um - it was fine. Nothing special. Never had my own room, though," I say, trying to laugh a bit.

"Oh." Josh is silent for a moment as he looks around my room. Eventually, his eyes land on the twin bed that sits across from mine. Hesitantly, he gives me an inquiring look - and for some reason, I know exactly what he's going to say before the words leave his mouth. "Mark? Could I - sleep in here?"

I sigh and give Josh a small, relenting smile. "Okay."

CHAPTER ELEVEN
TIM

Sitting at a comfortable booth in Red's Diner, I sink down in my chair, hidden from all eyes around me. I've been sitting for only five minutes, but it's felt much longer. I've already destroyed my straw wrapper, twisted two napkins into shreds, and drank half of my glass of water (although my mouth still feels dry).

As the seconds pass, I rack my mind for things to talk about with Kate. I can ask her questions about school, and her family - she seems to have a lot to say about them. In fact, she seems to have a lot to say about *anything* - so if I can keep her talking, I may never have to say much about myself.

Just then, the door opens, and I look up suddenly, the way I have every time someone's entered the restaurant for the past five minutes. But this time, I'm not disappointed. I watch as Kate walks into the restaurant. Her eyes wander for a minute, and I know she's looking for me. I straighten up, clear my throat, and wave, forcing a smile onto my face. Kate's green eyes land on me, and her face lights up.

I take a deep breath as she walks over, adjusting the purse hanging on her shoulder. I take a moment to observe her. Today, she's wearing a blue sweatshirt and acid-washed jeans, and she's wearing her strawberry-blonde hair in a high ponytail. Her large hoop earrings swing as she approaches the booth, and her eyeshadow sparkles under the bright lights of the restaurant.

"Hi," she says, sitting down across from me. "How are you?"

I swallow hard. My mouth still feels dry. "Hi. Good; how are you?"

"I'm good." Kate takes a moment to look at the remnants of my straw wrapper and my half-drank glass of water. Suddenly, her face is clouded with concern. "Have - have you been waiting long?"

I shake my head quickly. "No, no. Just a few minutes. I got here early."

"Oh." Kate's face brightens just in time for a waitress to come over with another glass of water. "Look, here's -"

Kate stops suddenly as she looks up at the waitress. "Susan?"

The waitress, a tall girl with bouncing, permed blonde hair and dark blue eyes, looks at Kate in surprise. "Hey! What's going on?" she asks as she sets down a glass of water for Kate.

Kate looks at me and smiles, and then she looks back at the girl. "Uh, this is Tim. He's new in town. Tim, this is my cousin, Susan."

I raise my eyebrows as I realize that this is my first time meeting one of Kate's family members. "Oh, hi."

Susan flashes me a pearly-white smile and tosses her blonde hair. "Hi." She turns towards Kate and gives her what she must think is a subtle look. I glance away quickly and pretend not to notice.

Eventually, I look back to see Susan watching me. "Well - I'll leave you be. See you later, Kate. Nice to meet you, Tim," she says, walking away.

Kate waits until Susan is out of earshot. Finally, she says, "I didn't know she was working here. We haven't gotten to talk much lately, what with school and things. She's a junior, so we don't have any classes together."

I nod. "Oh."

There's a moment of silence as Kate takes the new glass of water and sticks a straw in it, swirling it around. I'm surprised at her silence; although I haven't known her for long, she couldn't seem to stop talking last time we saw each other.

Quickly resolving to fix this strange awkwardness, I clear my throat and ask, "So, do you have a big family?"

Kate looks up, her face full of gratitude. "Yeah, pretty big. Well, there's my parents, my brother and I. Then there's Susan, her parents, and both of my sets of grandparents, who all live around here. Then there's my cousins, aunt and uncle who live in Kentucky."

I wait until Kate finishes explaining her family tree and I smile as I notice the eager, flushed look on her face. I've never known a person more excited to simply talk about life. Her energy is infectious, and once she asks me the same question that I asked her, I hastily reply.

"No, my family isn't big," I say. "It's just my parents and me. I don't have any living extended family."

The lie leaves my mouth before I can stop it. Kate nods understandingly. "Ah. Well, maybe you'd like that better than having a big family. I mean, when my family gets together for Thanksgiving, Christmas, or Easter, it's hard to get a word in edgewise. So, you learn to talk fast and loudly from a young age. I guess that's why I'm such a chatterbox," blushes Kate.

I grin. "I wish I had a big family like that. It sounds fun."

"Well, I'm sure you were able to get a lot more attention from your parents when you were little," says Kate, taking a sip of water.

I shrug as my mind begins racing for something else to say. "So - what's your brother like?"

Kate thinks for a moment, tilting her head and letting her reddish ponytail fall over her shoulder. "He's older than me by a couple years. He's a sophomore in college. I'd say we're pretty similar; we both like sports, especially basketball. We both like music. I have a large record collection, half of which came from him when he moved to college. He's going there to pursue a degree in music."

"That's cool. What instruments does he play?"

"Oh, everything. Piano, guitar, violin - even the saxophone."

"Can you play any instruments?"

Kate nods. "Just the piano. My parents made me take lessons in elementary and middle school. I don't take lessons anymore, but I remember how to play. Andy wanted me to keep it up; when we were younger, he always talked about starting a band."

I raise my eyebrows. "Who's Andy?"

Kate laughs. "Oh, I'm sorry. That's my brother. Anyways, I'll never be as good at music as him, so I don't practice much. I'm better at singing than anything else."

Suddenly, Kate looks at me and shakes her head. "Oh gosh, I'm sorry. I feel like I've been doing all the talking. I told you I was a chatterbox."

About to panic, I shake my head. "No, no, it's okay. I like listening."

"But I don't know anything about you. Do you like music?"

I nod. "Yeah, sure."

"Do you play any instruments?"

Shaking my head, I think back to the last dance I attended, when I saw Matt play with his band. Even though I could never imagine myself getting up on stage, I remember feeling rare twinges of regret when I watched Matt play. He was one of the most popular guys in school, he had a girlfriend, and he had as much fame as a seventeen-year-old guy from a small town could get in high school. "Nah. I was sort of a band manager for a couple years, though."

Kate smiles. "Oh, yeah?"

"Yeah." I sit up straighter, trying to appear confident. "My friend Matt had a band. He was constantly getting gigs at school and stuff like that."

Kate's green eyes widen in excitement. "Wow. That's totally something I'd love to do - be in a band, I mean. Maybe Andy and I *will* start one when he gets out of college."

I grin. "You should."

CHAPTER TWELVE
TIM

About an hour later, Kate and I stand up from the booth, our plates clean. "Well - it was great getting to talk to you, Tim," says Kate, slinging her purse back over her shoulder.

"Yeah, you too, Kate," I smile. "We'll have to do it again sometime."

"Totally." Kate turns to go, but she suddenly turns around and looks at me. "Hey, where do you live? I never asked that. Do you live near downtown?"

I nod quickly, unsure of what else to say. "Yeah. Makes it easy to get to work every day."

Kate nods. To my relief, she doesn't ask any more questions. "I bet. Well, bye, Tim."

I wave as she walks away and out the door. "Bye, Kate."

As soon as she's gone, I rush over to the public pay phone that sits in a corner of the restaurant. I drop a quarter into the slot. Thankfully, it isn't too loud for me to hear into the phone, but just loud enough so that no one around me can hear what I'm saying. Dialing Matt's number, I pick up the phone and hope that he'll be the one to answer.

"Hello?" says a voice on the other line. I breathe a sigh of relief; it's undoubtedly Matt.

"Hey, it's me," I say. "Don't say anything to make your mom suspicious."

"Oh, hey, Jack. What's up?" says Matt immediately in an overly excited voice.

"Good, good. Thanks."

"Wait a minute." There's silence for a moment. Then, Matt's voice returns to normal. "Okay, my mom just took Sarah with her to the store. Tim, how're you doin'? I didn't think I'd hear from you for a while."

"I know - but I figured it was safe to call and check in. What's the situation with the Fishers like? What happened after I left?"

"Well, they notified the police the morning after you left. They didn't do any searching themselves, though. All they did was stop by my house to ask if I'd seen you."

I feel my heart stop for an instant. "What'd you say?"

"I said 'no,' of course, doofus. You think I'd blow your cover just like that? I told them I had no idea where you were and that I hadn't seen you in a while."

"And they believed you?"

"Of course! I can be a good actor when I wanna be."

"So they weren't that concerned?"

Matt sighs. "Tim, if you really thought they'd be concerned, would you have run away in the first place? I think they would've encouraged you to see your brother a long time ago if they cared."

Although I already know all this, Matt's words still hurt, as they bring back all my painful memories from the past few years. "Yeah. I know."

"So, where are you?"

I look around the restaurant for a moment and feel a smile spreading across my face. "Davidson."

"Tim, that's only a couple of hours away. It's been over a week; I thought you'd reached Charlotte by now."

I bite my lip. "Yeah, so did I - but my bike tire got punctured. I stayed in town to earn the money to buy another one. And then..." I let my voice trail off as I picture Kate Woodland's smiling face.

"Tim?" says Matt in a tone of voice that hints he knows what I'm thinking. "What happened?"

"Well... I met a girl."

To my surprise, Matt begins laughing. "A *girl*? You run away to find your brother and decide that now is a good time to get a girlfriend?"

I groan. "She's *not* my girlfriend. We've just talked a couple of times."

"What's she like?"

I hesitate. I've never spilled any sorts of romantic thoughts to anyone before - especially not Matt. But why wouldn't he understand? After all, he has a girlfriend.

"She's beautiful. She's got big, green eyes, and she talks a lot. She comes from a large family. She loves music."

Matt laughs again. "Sounds like I should meet this girl."

70

I frown. "*Matt*," I say in a disapproving tone.

"Okay, okay. You know I'm kidding. Anne and I are still together - and not breaking up anytime soon."

"Well, good."

"So - are you gonna ask her out?"

"I sort of already did. I mean, we ate dinner together tonight, but it wasn't like a real date or anything. I know that, and she knows that. But I want to ask her out for real sometime."

Matt lets out a low, soft whistle. "Gee, Tim, you sure know how to plan a trip. Never thought you'd be the kind of guy to let your head get turned by a girl."

"Well, it's happened before. I've just never had the guts to ask a girl out, is all. Not on a *real* date, anyways."

"You think she's really special, then?"

I sigh. "Yeah. Yeah, she is."

"Well, what you need to do is -" Matt stops suddenly. Then I hear him yell, "Yeah, I'm in here."

"What's goin' on?" I ask, my voice suddenly at a whisper.

"I've gotta go. Call me again sometime, alright?" With that, the phone hangs up, leaving me standing in Red's Diner with a thousand thoughts on my mind - and no one to tell them to.

CHAPTER THIRTEEN
MARK

I open my eyes slowly, and I sit up groggily. For a moment, I forget where I am, and I have to remind myself of yesterday's events. Then, I remember what my first order of business is: I need to find a job.

Looking around for a moment, I expect to see Josh sleeping in his bed across from mine, but he's not there. I scan the entire room in vain; Josh is nowhere in sight.

I begin to panic. Josh knows that he shouldn't wander around without me - doesn't he?

Throwing off the bedcovers and standing up, I turn on my heels and run down the hallway. "Josh? Josh?" I yell.

"Over here," a small voice calls.

My eyes widen, and I turn in the direction of the voice. I walk into the living room and find Josh sitting on the floor, staring out the window, watching a few brightly colored birds sitting on the windowsill. When he sees me, he turns and smiles at me - but I'm not really in a smiling mood.

"Josh, what're you doing out here?" I ask, crossing my arms and looking down at him in what I hope is an authoritative way.

Suddenly, Josh looks confused, and even nervous. "I just wanted to sit down by the window. What's wrong?"

72

"Well, I didn't know where you were! You can't -" I stop, realizing how I sound. I don't want Josh to think that I was scared, and afraid at the thought of him being missing. "Just - don't wander off. We need to stay undercover. Okay?"

Josh nods, and I let out a sigh of relief. Although I was the one who suggested we stay in the cabin, part of me can't help but feel worried that we'll be discovered. It's one thing for us to stay in this town, but it's another to be living in someone else's house. Still, it's our best option, and I figured we can stay here until someone comes to kick us out.

"So - what are we doing today?" asks Josh, letting his eyes wander back to the two cardinals sitting on the window-sill.

I sit down on the couch and lean forward, my hands clasped together. "Well, I've gotta find a job."

Josh tears his gaze away from the birds and gives me a concerned look. Surprised by this reaction, I fold my arms across my chest in a defensive way. "What?"

"Have you ever had a job before?"

I clear my throat and stare out the window, avoiding Josh's gaze. "Well - no."

Josh suddenly looks even more worried than before. "Oh."

I rub my face with my hand and sigh. "It'll be fine. I know that I may not have a good chance of finding a job, but I have to try, don't I?"

Josh nods eagerly. "Yes, yes. And - I can help you. We can look for jobs together."

I smile. "Sure." I'm about to suggest we head to town immediately when I get a closer look at Josh. His pale face is covered in a layer of dirt. On impulse, I stand up and walk to the bathroom to get a look at myself in the mirror.

I'm immediately confronted with a pale, skinny, dirt-covered reflection. My straight, dark hair is matted, and there are dark circles around my eyes, courtesy of the several sleep-less nights I've had for the past many days that Josh and I were traveling.

With a sigh, I conclude that I won't be able to get a job anywhere looking the way I do now. Walking out to the living room, I tell Josh that I'm getting washed up, and that afterwards, we can go job hunting.

* * * * * * * * * *

After I take a shower and comb my hair, I wash our clothes while Josh showers. Now, we're walking down the main road near the cabin, keeping our eyes open for any "help wanted" signs. The further we walk, the busier the streets seem to get, with traffic becoming more congested and more buildings appearing.

Eventually, we reach what I assume is the downtown area of what I now know is the town of Andersonville, thanks to a sign we saw a little while ago. Walking past multiple res-taurants and other assorted shops, we stop walking in front of a fast-food restaurant. I glance down at Josh, who seems to be taking in his surroundings. "Well. This looks alright," I say. Josh nods slowly, and the two of us walk inside the restaurant.

Thankfully, only a few customers are present, sitting at the back of the restaurant. I realize that this is because it's not yet lunchtime. Breathing a sigh of relief, I step up to the counter, Josh at my side.

Standing at the counter, I observe the tall, dark haired young man standing across from me who appears to be in his mid-twenties. I wait for him to greet me, but he seems distracted by the book sitting on one side of the counter. After a few seconds, I clear my throat. This seems to startle him, and he looks at me with an apologetic expression.

"Oh, hey, I'm sorry," he says, laughing sheepishly. "What can I -"

Suddenly, the man looks at me in surprise. I see a strange, quizzical look flash across his face for a moment. "Excuse me - what's your name?" he asks.

I panic immediately and say the first name that hops off my tongue. "Mike."

The man's eyebrows raise, and he shrugs. "Oh. That's funny, I - I guess I just thought you were someone else."

Swallowing hard, I know exactly what this man must be thinking. He must have recognized me from a missing person ad that the foster home undoubtedly sent to the newspaper. Realizing that he could recognize Josh from an ad, as well, I say quickly, "And this is Tom. My brother."

The man looks down at Josh and gives him a friendly smile. "Hey there."

I begin talking quickly, trying to act casual. "Well, we're new in town, and I was kind of wondering if there's any jobs open around here. Do you know of any?"

The man bites his lip and shakes his head regretfully. "I'm sorry - there's no openings over here. As for the rest of town, I don't know. But I haven't seen many 'help wanted' signs around recently."

I can feel my face fall. "Oh. Well, that's okay. Thanks anyways."

The man smiles and waves as we walk away. "See you."

* * * * * * * * * *

Back in the cabin, Josh is sitting on the couch eating some cereal out of the box, and I'm pacing back and forth in the hallway, trying to think of some sort of job I can acquire without an interview. Something easy - something that a thirteen-year-old guy can do. By now, it's almost three o'clock, and I still haven't gotten any ideas.

Suddenly, I hear a noise coming from the living room, and I find Josh sitting on the couch, a small pile of cereal on the ground. "Whoops," he says apologetically.

"That's okay," I say quickly. "I'll clean it up." Walking back to the hallway, I open a closet door to look for a broom - and just as my eyes land on a mop and bucket, that's when it hits me: *I can wash cars*. It's something easy that Josh can help me with, and it'll earn us a good amount of money.

Rushing back to Josh, I look at him with a grin on my face. "Josh, I've got it."

Josh smiles - and just like that, I know my plan is going to work.

* * * * * * * * * *

Josh and I walk through a small neighborhood, keeping our eyes peeled for dirty-looking cars. Although it's almost October, the sun is beating down hard on us, making me wipe a few drops of sweat from my forehead.

Just then, I feel a tug on my sleeve, and I look to see Josh pointing to the right. "There's one!"

Sure enough, Josh has spotted one of the dirtiest looking cars I've ever seen. Although I can tell its original color was red, it's hard to tell through the thick layers of dirt and dust that the car has acquired.

Josh and I walk up to the front door, and I stretch out my arm, about to ring the doorbell - but I stop suddenly. Josh looks at me inquiringly, one eyebrow raised. "What's wrong?"

I wring my hands anxiously and shrug. "I'm - I'm not good at talking to people. I don't wanna screw something up."

Josh stares at me. "But you did just fine talking to that man at the restaurant."

I shake my head. "That was rare - and it was mostly out of instinct. I just hate talking to people. What should I say?"

Josh seems a little surprised that I'm asking him for advice, but he doesn't hesitate to reply. "Well, first you say hello."

I nod slowly. "Yeah. Then what?"

"Then, you say your name and ask if the person would like a car wash."

I wait for him to say something more, but he doesn't. "That's it?" That can't be it.

"That's it."

Huh. Maybe this is simpler than I thought. Maybe I'm just overthinking everything. I mean, I haven't talked very much in the past three years, and I've never made a sales pitch before, so I guess I'm rightfully nervous about this - but still. "Okay, then," I say, taking a deep breath. "Here goes." The two of us take a few more steps up to the front porch, and then I knock on the door. I almost want to turn and run away, but I can't do that. I can't be a coward.

After a moment's silence, the door slowly creaks open, and a middle-aged, dark-haired woman emerges. She doesn't say anything; she seems to be waiting for me to begin the conversation.

"Oh, uh, hello," I say.

The woman nods in greeting. "Hello," she says.

"My name is Mike. Mike Richardson," I say, thinking fast. "And I just noticed that your car could use a wash."

The woman lets out a little laugh at this and fixes her neon-blue-colored headband which is sliding off her head. "Yes, I know," she says. "I've just been very busy."

"Well, would you like me to wash it for you?"

The woman raises her eyebrows. "For - money?"

"Yes."

"How much?"

"Uh, two dollars."

I wait anxiously as the woman thinks about this. She glances at her car, then at me. Then she notices Josh. "Who's this?" she asks.

"Oh, this is my brother, Tom," I say.

"Would he help you wash the car?" asks the woman.

I hesitate, surprised at this question. "Oh. Um, yeah, he would help me."

"And where is your home? I don't believe I've ever met your parents."

Ugh. Why do people like to ask so many questions? "Well, we just moved here, so I can't remember our address," I say apologetically. "But we do live in Andersonville."

"Hm. Okay. Well, when would you wash the car?"

"Today, if that's alright."

"Yes, of course. Um - do you need any supplies? Like some sponges and rags, or soap?"

I nod. "Yes, some sponges and rags would be great. We've got a bucket and soap already, though."

The woman smiles, says goodbye, and closes the door. A few moments later, she returns with a few sponges. "The hose is on the side of the house. I'll see you later, boys." With that, she heads back inside.

Victorious, I turn and begin walking across the driveway. I feel so elated that as I fill the bucket with water, I don't notice the look that Josh is giving me. When I do, I frown. "What? What's wrong?" I ask.

Josh sighs as we walk over to the car and begin soaping it up with our sponges. "Nothing really, I guess."

"Then why are you looking at me like that?"

Josh hesitates, and lowering his voice, he says, "Well - because you really lied to that woman."

I shake my head, not understanding. "What are you talking about? We lied about our names earlier."

"I guess so - but I'm not sure it's such a good idea. Shouldn't we just tell the truth? It can't hurt."

I'm ready to respond hastily, but Josh's eyes are so full of worry that I stop and try to think of something better to say than, *So what?*

"Well, Josh, it's not that bad. I had to say something to stop her from asking so many questions. I mean, it's crazy how many questions adults ask! They don't make any sense."

I guess that wasn't a great response, either, but it's what came out.

"But they do make sense! She just wanted to know where we lived," exclaims Josh, obviously bothered by my careless attitude.

I turn quickly, almost knocking over the water-filled bucket. "What do you think would have happened if we'd told her, Josh? She would have found out who we were and that we're living in a cabin because we don't have any place else to live, and she would have sent us back to Charlotte. And I'm not going back there *ever*. Do you understand?" I say all of this in such a harsh tone that Josh seems to shrink back. I kind of regret this - but what I don't regret is the understanding look that is now on Josh's face.

"Yeah. I understand," he says.

Hesitantly, I reach out and give Josh a pat on the shoulder, soapy water dripping from my hand. I almost want to apologize for my previous actions - but I feel incapable of saying "sorry." So, I just say, "Everything's gonna be fine. You'll see."

Josh gives me a small smile, as if to say that he understands the meaning behind my words, and I give him a grateful smile back.

CHAPTER FOURTEEN
MARK

After about an hour of cleaning the dirty car, it finally returns to its original, shiny red color. Josh and I exchange a satisfied look as we finish drying off the car. Then, the two of us bound up to the front door, where the woman just happens to be standing, obviously waiting for us.

"Well, boys," she says with an approving smile, "you've done a great job."

Josh and I wait patiently as the woman reaches into her pocket with a flour-covered hand. The next thing I know, she's handing me not two, but *four* one-dollar bills.

I stare at the money in astonishment for a moment before mustering enough courage to say, "Oh, ma'am, this is too much." I hold out the extra money, knowing that to refuse it is the right thing to do.

The woman shakes her head of dark hair and pushes my hand away. "No, no - you said two dollars, and I take that to mean two dollars *each*. You boys are obviously very hard workers, and that car was certainly overdue for a wash. Please take the money."

I grin and don't hesitate to retract my arm. "Thanks a lot," I grin.

The woman smiles. "You're welcome."

With that, Josh and I walk off down the street, significantly richer (and wetter) than we were an hour ago. Part of me wants to save the money - but the other part is able only to listen to my stomach.

Turning to Josh, I say, "What do you say we stop by a restaurant?"

Josh hesitates for a moment as he stares at the money in my hand. Then, he too lets his stomach get the better of him, and he nods. "Yeah. Let's go!"

The two of us begin walking a little faster, the promise of food propelling us to move forward despite our aching feet. We've just about reached the downtown area when Josh stops walking suddenly.

I stop and stare at him quizzically. "What's wrong?"

Josh doesn't answer. I follow his gaze and realize that his eyes have landed on a park about ten feet away. The sounds of children laughing and playing have already reached my ears, but I didn't think much of them. The look on Josh's face appears to be that of fascination.

"Mark," he says quietly, "could we - could we go over there?"

I raise my eyebrows in surprise. "You don't want to eat?"

Josh hesitates and looks back and forth between the park and I. "Well - yes. I do. But - oh, could we please go over there? Just for a little while?"

I stare at the park for a moment. It's filled with people, and not the safest place for Josh and I to be, especially with adults around. Besides, my stomach is growling, and I don't want to wait another minute to eat. But Josh looks so innocent and hopeful that I can't say no.

"Oh - okay. Just for a little while, if you say your name is Tom," I relent.

Josh's face lights up immediately. "Thanks, Mark." Excitedly, he takes me by the hand and drags me to the park. I watch as the little boy climbs to the top of the slide, a grin on his face. Suddenly, I wonder if Josh has ever been to a large playground like this one before. He's only seven years old, and he lived in a foster home and with different foster families for most of his life - so I'm guessing that the answer is: not often.

Suddenly, I hear someone yell, "Robbie!" I look to my right just in time to jump out of the way of a little boy flying past me. A girl about my age catches up a second later, breathing hard. "Robbie, you get back here right now!" she yells. Suddenly, she notices me, and she winces. "Sorry," she says, her voice suddenly at a normal level. "My brother and I need to get home now, and he isn't listening."

I can't remember the last time I talked to a girl my age. In fact, it's been a while now since I've talked to *anyone* my age. But I rub the back of my neck and force myself to reply, "Uh, that's okay. Do you need any help?"

"Yeah, that would be nice," she replies breathlessly. "Let's try to corner him." She runs one way, and I run the other. Immediately, I spot the little boy - but he's not running anymore. In fact, he's perched up on top of the playground, talking to Josh.

Seeing this, I grab hold of the playground and swing up to them. "Jo - *Tom*, who's this?" I ask as the two kids notice me.

"This is Robbie," says Josh, immediately jumping in to introduce his new friend.

"Hey, Robbie," I say, nodding to the little boy.

Robbie gives me a little wave. "Hi."

Just then, I notice Robbie's older sister creeping up behind him, a mischievous look on her face, and she grabs him around the stomach. "No!" yells Robbie. Josh gives me a concerned look, but it disappears when he sees that the two siblings are laughing.

"Robert Taylor, don't you *dare* run off like that again!" says the girl, obviously frustrated but amused at the same time.

"Okay, but look!" replies Robbie, wriggling out of his sister's arms and changing the subject skillfully. "I made a new friend! This is Tom."

The girl freezes, as if she almost forgot that she and her brother weren't alone, and she straightens up and brushes off her oversized, neon pink sweatshirt and skinny jeans. "Hey, Tom," she says with a smile.

"Hi," says Josh.

The girl looks at me, then at Josh, then at me again. "Do you two know each other?" she asks.

85

"Yeah, Tom's my brother," I say easily, ruffling Josh's red hair.

"Oh, I see. And what's your name?" asks the girl.

For some reason, I have an urge to tell this girl my real name - but I end up saying, "Mike," as naturally as I can. "What's yours?"

"April," answers the girl, tucking her golden hair behind her ear.

"Nice to meet you," I say.

"You too," replies April, her smile growing wider.

Robbie clears his throat, and the two of us look at him. "April, I thought we've gotta go home."

April laughs shyly as her cheeks turn a deeper shade of pink. "Um - yeah. Well - it was nice to meet you, Mike."

"Yeah, you too. Maybe I'll see you around," I say smoothly.

April nods and gives Josh a little wave. "Bye, Tom."

Josh smiles and replies, "Bye."

The two siblings turn, and we watch as Robbie jumps off of the playground, and then April after him. I watch them run all the way down the street, April's laughter still ringing in my ears.

* * * * * * * * * *

Arriving in the downtown area of Andersonville, I walk a little faster, eager to get some food in my stomach.

Josh must notice my quicker pace because he begins jogging to keep up with me.

"Where are we going to eat?" asks Josh, looking incredulously at the countless restaurants that we pass as we walk, with their perfectly arranged window boxes and waiters with spotless uniforms.

I shrug. "The cheapest place we can find." Suddenly, my eyes land on the fast-food restaurant that Josh and I entered earlier in the day, where we talked to the man about finding a job. "There," I say, pointing straight ahead. "Come on."

Josh and I jog down the sidewalk and enter the restaurant, the smell of fries immediately flooding my nose. Although I'd like to rush eagerly up to the counter and order right away, I try to maintain a sense of calm as I force myself to walk slowly.

I wait in line for a moment, allowing the couple ahead of Josh and I to finish ordering. Once they sit down at one of the few vacant tables left, I'm greeted by a young woman with black hair. A few beads of sweat are glistening on her forehead, thanks to the obvious heat of the kitchen.

"Hi," she says with a smile. "What can I get you today?"

I give the menu a quick glance before ordering a burger and fries for myself. Then, I let Josh order for himself, as well. Once we're finished, the two of us find a vacant booth and sit down. I feel too impatient to wait for my food, so I concentrate on staring at other people's plates, too hungry to think about anything else.

It's only been five minutes before the young man from earlier in the day walks over with our food, a grin on his face. "Well, if it isn't Mr. Job Hunter and his partner. Did you find some work?"

I smile and resist the urge to dig in right away. However, this doesn't hinder Josh, as he begins to scarf down his burger with a look of excitement on his face. I suppress a laugh and reply, "Yeah, actually."

The young man looks closely at me for a moment. "I don't mean to seem nosy or anythin', but - you seem kinda young to be looking for a job."

I shrug and let the lies begin to fly off my tongue. "Oh, well, it wasn't as if I was looking for a *real* job. I mean, I just wanted to make some extra money. So, Tom and I decided to wash cars."

The young man nods. "Oh. I see."

Suddenly, Josh looks up from his food and cocks his head. "What's your name?"

The young man looks surprised for a split second, but he doesn't hesitate to answer. "Steven."

Josh sticks out his hand, and Steven takes it, giving it a shake. "Nice to meet you," says Josh.

Steven grins. "Nice to meet you, too, Tom." He looks back at me and nods. "Welcome to town, guys." With that, he walks off, leaving Josh and I to enjoy our food.

CHAPTER FIFTEEN
TIM

Running out of the YMCA, I narrowly avoid tripping over a large branch lying across the sidewalk. Hopping over it, I keep running, and I don't stop until I reach the woods, where I left my bike. The journey back to town is a bit longer, considering I have to lug my bike along with me, but I quicken my pace when my eyes finally land on a bike shop. It stands there with its shining, spotless windows, and bikes for display, as if it's been waiting for me all this time.

Eagerly, I step up to the front counter and am greeted by a tall, middle-aged man with graying brown hair and a curious expression. "Hi," I say excitedly. "Um, I'm here for a bike tire."

The man nods slowly. "What kind?"

I shrug. "Well - here, this is my bike."

The man steps forward and begins examining the bike and its punctured tire. Quickly, I begin to explain. "I was riding it and accidentally ran over a nail."

I'm answered by nothing but silence. I wait another moment before asking, "So, what do you think? Can you get it to me today?"

The man stands up slowly and shakes his head. "I'm sorry, but I'm going to have to special order it."

I can feel my smile vanish in an instant. "What? Are - are you sure?"

The man nods. "Yep."

I wring my hands. "Well - how long will it take to get it? A couple days?"

The man looks at me over his glasses. "At least a week. I can keep your bike here for you and change the tire when it comes, though."

I take a deep breath. I was *not* expecting this. What I *was* expecting was to get my bike tire today, arrive in Charlotte by tomorrow morning, and leave with my brother by tomorrow night. In a matter of hours, we'd be together again. Now, it'll be a whole other week - maybe even more.

My mouth begins moving automatically. "Alright. I'll - I'll check back in a week, then."

The man says goodbye, but I barely hear him. I walk out of the store, feeling numb. Although this time to earn extra money could be a good thing, I was ready to bike out of Davidson today - not a week from now.

Frustrated, I'm just about to collapse on the nearest bench when I hear a sweet, familiar voice. "Tim?"

I look up to see Kate rushing towards me. Immediately, a half-genuine smile appears on my face. "Hi," I say as Kate approaches me.

"What're you doing?" she asks, observing the disappointed look on my face.

I shrug and sigh. "Well, I just ordered a new bike tire. The man at the shop said it'd take at least a week to get here."

Kate gives me a look of concern. "I'm sorry."

I suppress the urge to explain what exactly she's saying sorry for, and instead I say, "Yeah, well, it's alright." Suddenly, I notice that Kate is dressed even nicer than usual. She's wearing a knee-length, light green dress, and her hair is curled.

"What're you all dressed up for?" I ask.

Kate looks down at herself, then back at me. "Oh, my family just came from church."

I nod. "Oh."

Kate opens her mouth to say something, but she closes it just as quickly. Finally, after looking at me for a moment, she asks, "Have you seen much of town yet?"

I shake my head and stare at the sidewalk, where it seems the whole town is walking, bringing Davidson to life on a previously quiet Sunday.

Kate smiles. "You said you like music, right?"

I nod, and Kate begins walking down the sidewalk, motioning for me to follow her. "Come on!"

I follow her down the busy streets, walking single file behind her, thanks to how congested the sidewalk is. Finally, she stops, and I'm able to stand next to her. "What're we doing?" I ask.

Kate points straight ahead of her, and I follow her finger. Suddenly, I realize that we're standing in front of a shop called, "Davidson Music Store."

Walking through the front door, Kate and I are immediately greeted by the sound of "Burning Heart" by Survivor, making me think of when I saw *Rocky 4* in theaters last year. I stand at the front of the store for a moment, taking in the walls which are lined with records and cassettes. I let out a low whistle, and Kate grins.

"Isn't it rad?" she asks, following me as I begin browsing the records. "It's all the music you could ever want. They have all the latest stuff, which is why it's my favorite store. I think I've bought almost every record I have from here. I don't really buy cassette tapes - do you?"

I stop browsing for a moment to shake my head. Kate nods. "Good. I just think records are more - well, *fun*. I have a Walkman, but my grandma gave me my first record when I was eight, and I just learned to prefer the sound. Do you have lots of records?"

I shake my head. "I used to. I haven't gotten around to buying many lately, though." My fingers fly nimbly through the stacks of records, and I don't stop until my eyes land on the name "AC/DC."

Gently, I pull the record out and stare at it, my eyes skimming through all the song titles. Kate, who's looking over my shoulder, asks, "Do you like them?"

I shrug. "Yeah. They were my bro - *my* favorite band for a while."

Kate nods, and she's silent for a moment before letting out an excited squeal. "Oh, it's here!" She rushes over to the other side of the store. I follow her and watch as she picks up a Steve Winwood album in excitement. "I knew it'd show up at some point."

She looks up for a moment and sees me smiling. Blushing, she says, "Give me one second." She walks up to the counter, and a few minutes later, we're walking down the street again, Kate carrying her new album in a shopping bag. The sun is pouring down on us, making her hair look golden.

"Well," she says, "I'd better head home now. I told my parents I'd only be a few minutes."

"Oh," I reply. "I'll see you later, then."

I expect her to walk away, but she doesn't. Instead, she asks, "Wanna walk with me?"

I swallow hard. "To - your house?"

Kate nods. "Sure. You can meet my parents."

As much as I hate this idea, Kate looks so earnest and excited that before I know what I'm doing, I say, "Okay."

* * * * * * * * * *

It's only been about ten minutes when Kate announces, "This is it."

I look up at the house we're standing in front of. It's small and cozily situated in a suburban neighborhood near downtown Davidson. I observe its two large windows at the front, with flower boxes on the outside of these windows. The boxes are filled with different colored daisies, miraculously holding onto life in the last few days of September.

Walking up to the front door, which is painted white, I almost want to run - but I can't risk disappointing Kate. So I take a deep breath and step into the house.

"Mom, I'm home," yells Kate. She takes off her shoes and walks down the hallway, disappearing. I take a moment to look around the house. Straight in front of me is a closet, a bit of white paint peeling at the edges.

To my left is a staircase, where two old pictures hang on the wall. One is of Kate, and I assume that the other, which features a boy with reddish hair and green eyes identical to Kate's, is her brother Andy. The fact that the photos are old makes me realize that Andy must look a bit different and older now, and I marvel over how young Kate looks in her photo; she can't be more than thirteen years old.

"Tim?" a voice says. I whirl around to see Kate standing in front of me, her eyebrows raised. "Come on, my dad's out picking up lunch, but my mom's in the kitchen."

I nod and follow her down the hallway, which opens to reveal a small kitchen, where a tall woman with blonde hair is standing. "Hi," she says, dusting off her flour-covered hands. "Tim, right? Nice to meet you."

I force a smile. "Nice to meet you, too."

I study Mrs. Woodland's face for a moment. Her green eyes are where Kate must get hers - but other than this trait, the two of them don't look very much alike.

"So, you're new to town?" asks Mrs. Woodland, turning back to the kitchen counter and mixing a bowl which I guess is banana bread, thanks to the many banana peels sitting in the garbage.

"Yeah," I say half absentmindedly, still taking in the house.

"Are your parents feeling settled in yet?"

I start for a moment, surprised at this question - and then I remember. I lied to Kate yesterday. I told her I was an only child who'd just moved to town with my parents. She must have passed on this information to her mom.

Nodding and thinking fast, I say, "Oh, yeah, they're doing fine. They're still busy though, so we haven't gotten to meet very many people yet. I doubt things will slow down for a while."

"Ah, I remember that feeling," says Mrs. Woodland with a smile, moving the batter into a pan. "Our family hasn't moved in years - and now I know why. It's a hassle, but once you get settled in, things get back to normal very quickly."

Mrs. Woodland takes a moment to observe me. Then, she asks, "What do you like to do for fun? You're tall - do you play basketball?"

I nod. "Yeah, I do. It's fun."

"My son is tall, too, but he doesn't play. He gets his height from his dad. Do you get your height from your parents?"

I nod again. "Uh huh. Um - my dad's pretty tall." Suddenly, before I know what I'm doing, words are flying out of my mouth - and I know they aren't true. "My dad played basketball with me a lot when I was a kid. I guess I got it from him." The convincing tone I take on as I say these words almost makes me believe them myself. Then, I feel the urge to say something that's true, to make up for the lies - so I do. "I don't look much like my dad, though. People have always said I look a lot like my mom."

Mrs. Woodland nods and smiles, as if she's simply processing all this information. Then, she says, "You know, I'd love to meet them sometime. Your parents, I mean."

I begin stammering. "Oh, uh - yeah, that would be great, but - well, they won't be free for a while. Still busy with the house and everything, you know. My dad's been making lots of repairs."

Nervous, I find myself staring at the oven. Mrs. Woodland seems to notice, because she asks, "Would you like to stay a while for some banana bread?"

I snap back to attention quickly. It's time that I get out of here before I end up lying much more than I already have. "Oh, no, thank you," I say. "I've gotta head out and help my parents with some things. It was nice to meet you, though."

I turn to Kate and give her a smile. "Bye, Kate."

She returns my smile and watches as I walk down the hallway and out the door. "Bye, Tim."

CHAPTER SIXTEEN
TIM

It's Monday now, and I've been working non-stop all afternoon. Now, though, I'm exhausted and ready for the day to be over. I let the pasted smile on my face melt as soon as the clock turns to 5 PM. Giving Mr. Kilmer a wave, I head out the front door of the store - and run into Kate Woodland.

"Oh, man," I exclaim, laughing at my clumsiness. "Sorry, Kate. Almost ran into you again."

Kate laughs, some of her reddish hair falling into her face.

I clear my throat and cock my head curiously, leaning against the brick wall of the store. "So - what're you doin' here?"

A small smile appears on Kate's face, and she begins stammering. "Well - I wanted to give you an - what I mean is, I wanted to invite you to -"

I frown and lean down a bit to look her in the eye. "Kate? Is something wrong?"

Kate laughs again - but this time, I can sense a bit of nervousness in it. "No, no, nothing's wrong. Well - I wanted to invite you to come over for dinner at my house tomorrow night. Actually, *we* would like to invite you. That is, my family and I."

Surprised and amused, I grin. I couldn't be more nervous about the situation, but I would never pass up the opportunity to spend time with Kate. "Yeah, I'd love to."

Kate nods quickly as a smile flashes across her face. "Okay, great. I'll see you then." She turns away to go.

"Wait!" I exclaim. "What time should I come over?"

Kate stops in her tracks and turns around, her face sheepish. "Oh! Um - around five-thirty."

I nod and give her a thumbs-up. "I'll be there."

Kate smiles, and then she begins jogging, almost running into a bicyclist coming down the sidewalk. I shake my head in amusement and smile, my emotions a mix of happiness and terror.

* * * * * * * * * *

A few minutes before five-thirty the next night, I walk down the street with my hands in my pockets and my hair freshly combed, the early October breeze cooling me down some. Before I know it, I've reached Kate's street; thankfully, I remember the exact house.

Stepping up to the front door, I take a deep breath. I stare at my outstretched hand and shake my head. *Stop acting like a coward, Ryder.*

Knock knock. I step back from the door, waiting in anticipation to see Kate's eager face. But when the door opens, what I see instead is an unfamiliar face - the face of a guy who can't be more than a couple years older than me.

"You must be Tim. I've gotta say, man, you look relatively normal. What're you doin' hanging around with Kate for?"

Quickly, I clear my throat, but before I can answer, I'm interrupted by a familiar voice.

"Andy!" exclaims Kate as she comes rushing forward. The sight of her instantly calms my nerves. She gives the guy a painful-looking nudge in the side with her elbow and shakes her head. "I told you to tell me when Tim got here. I knew I shouldn't have let you answer the door."

The guy laughs, and I look closely at his features for a moment. Green eyes, reddish hair, and a big grin - this guy looks as if he could be Kate's twin.

"I see you've met my brother, Andy," she says.

"Oh, hi. Nice to meet you," I say, sticking out my hand eagerly.

Andy gives me a big, toothy smile and shakes my hand. "Nice to meet you, too. Come on in."

I step inside the house and am immediately greeted by an amazing smell. I give Kate a smile. "Smells great in here."

Kate tucks a strand of curled hair behind her ear and glances towards the kitchen, bouncing up and down nervously. "You do like Italian food, don't you?"

I nod quickly. "Oh, yeah, I love it."

A smile appears on Kate's face, and she nods. "Good. Well, come on in."

The three of us walk through the hallway, and Andy begins talking. "So, Tim, you're new in town, right? What do you think of Davidson so far?"

"Oh, it's great. It's - small."

"Not too small, though, right?"

I laugh and shake my head. "Nah. I like it."

Just as we step into the kitchen, I'm immediately met by Kate's mom, who rushes forward with a welcoming smile on her face. "Hi, Tim. How are you?"

"I'm good, Mrs. Woodland. How are you?"

"Just fine." At that moment, a tall, reddish-haired man steps forward, and Mrs. Woodland says, "Tim, this is my husband, Alan."

Mr. Woodland offers me his hand, and I give it a shake. "Welcome, Tim," he says, his voice firm and reassuring. "Kate's told us a lot about you."

I look over at Kate questioningly, and she laughs as she makes her way over to my side. "All good," she says.

Mrs. Woodland glances over her shoulder towards the dining room and then beckons us forward. "Well, the food's all ready, so let's eat."

I follow Mrs. Woodland out to the dining room, where the table is set with plates of chicken parmesan. Hesitantly taking my place on one side of the table, I watch as Kate wastes no time at all in sitting down on my right.

I wipe my hands on my jeans in preparation to begin cutting my chicken, but I'm interrupted by the voice of Mrs. Woodland. "Alan, will you pray?"

Mr. Woodland smiles, nods, and clears his throat. I watch as every member of the Woodland family bows their heads and clasps their hands together. Quickly, I do the same.

"Dear Lord," says Mr. Woodland, his voice calm and quiet, "we thank you for the food on this table, and the opportunity to share it with a new member of the community. Thank you for leading him and his family to this town, and for giving us the chance to meet someone new. Amen."

"Amen," repeats the other members of the Woodland family. I echo the response quietly and immediately begin cutting into my chicken, my palms suddenly sweating ten times more than before.

"So, Tim," says Andy after taking a sip of water, "what'd you move to Davidson for? You're a senior, right? Thinking about college?"

I open my mouth but don't answer. Seeing my hesitancy, Kate jumps in to explain. "Andy goes to Davidson College for school. He's always trying to get people to go there – it's like he's earning commission or something." With these last few words, Kate gives her brother a meaningful, annoyed look.

Andy laughs and throws his hands up in surrender. "I admit, I'm proud of my school - but I *don't* talk about it that much."

Kate shrugs and tries to appear serious, but a hint of a smile plays along her lips.

Ready to reply, I shake my head. "No, uh, I didn't move to Davidson for college - although it sounds like a good school. Um, my parents just wanted a change of scenery. We lived in Charlotte practically my whole life, and I guess they were just ready for a change. So was I."

Andy nods understandingly. I almost sigh in relief, happy to have answered one question without complications - but I wince when I hear Mr. Woodland ask, "Tim, do you go to Roosevelt High School? That's where Kate goes."

Shaking my head quickly, I let the words begin flying out of my mouth. "No, sir. I go to... Oh, what's the other school near here? I keep forgetting the name. It's, uh..." I snap my fingers, as if trying hard to remember the name.

"Jefferson," says Kate.

I nod quickly and look at her eagerly, as if a lightbulb has just gone off in my mind. Thankfully, part of me does remember having seen a school called "Jefferson" while I was walking through town the other day. "Yeah, yeah, that's it."

"Ah, so you must live on the other side of town," decides Mr. Woodland. "Since you're in the other district."

"Yep, that's where I live," I say, nodding firmly.

"How long do you think you'll be staying in town, Tim? Since college is coming up, and all," asks Mrs. Woodland.

I bite my lip and glance quickly at Kate's curious, eager face. Maybe this is a question I can answer honestly.

"Um - well, I will be leaving soon, to visit a few colleges. I may be gone for a while."

Kate's face falls quickly, and I immediately regret my answer. Mrs. Woodland smiles. "Oh, well that's good that you're preparing. College really sneaks up on you. I remember when Andy was getting ready. It feels like yesterday."

I nod, and to change the subject, I ask, "Kate, how's your new Steve Winwood album?"

* * * * * * * * * *

The rest of the dinner goes off without a hitch. At 7 PM, I glance up at the clock hanging on the Woodlands' wall and decide that it's time I left. I quickly voice this to Mr. and Mrs. Woodland, who thank me for coming over. I thank them for the invitation and say goodbye to Andy. Just as I'm about to say goodbye to Kate, though, she exclaims, "I'll walk you out."

I nod. "Okay."

I wave goodbye to the rest of the Woodlands as Kate and I walk down the hallway and out through the front door. Immediately, an orange glow is cast over us from the sunset. It casts a beautiful light on Kate's strawberry-blonde hair and makes her green eyes sparkle as she smiles up at me.

"Well," she says, "thanks for coming over."

I grin. "Thanks for inviting me. My parents have been so busy with the house that I haven't had a good meal like that in a long time."

Kate nods but doesn't say anything. For a long moment, we look into each other's eyes, both unsure of what to say, but sure that we don't want to say goodbye. Then, before I know what I'm doing, I ask, "Would you like to go out with me tomorrow night?"

I watch as Kate nods eagerly, flashes me one more smile, and walks inside her house, leaving me standing on the front step with a big grin on my face.

CHAPTER SEVENTEEN
MARK

I rub my hands together to keep them warm and watch out my bedroom window as the rain pours, pattering against the leaves. It's been three days now, and Josh and I have washed four cars. Altogether, though, we've knocked on the doors of *six* houses. Two turned us down fast. One owner was an older woman who barely cracked the door to listen to me speak. The other was a younger guy who was carrying a Walkman and looked too preoccupied to pay attention to us.

Although it was disappointing to waste so much time just to be turned down, these weren't huge setbacks, and Josh and I still ended up making plenty of money for food. Today, it's been raining, so we've had to stay inside. There isn't much to do in the house, but I've been enjoying the quiet.

Josh has been sitting in the living room, reading a book that he found on the bookshelf in another bedroom. He chose to read the unabridged version of *The Count of Monte Cristo*. I was surprised, especially when he said he'd read it once before. I couldn't help asking if he understood it, and I was even more surprised when he proceeded to explain the plot to me in detail. Since then, I haven't heard a peep from him.

Suddenly curious, I roll over on my bed and sit up. "Josh?" I yell. "Hey, Josh, you there?"

Nothing. I try again, louder this time. "Josh?"

All I can hear is my heart pounding in my ears. Without hesitating, I leap from my bed and rush down the hallway and into the living room. My eyes land on the back of the couch; there's no sign of Josh. Moving around to the front, I suddenly see him. He's lying on the couch, so small that I couldn't see him before, and his face looks pale and sickly.

My hands begin shaking. Forcing myself to take a step forward, I say his name one more time. "Josh?"

"Mark?" a small voice replies.

I stumble and drop down at Josh's side. "Yeah, I'm here. Are you okay?"

"N - no," whispers Josh, his green eyes barely open. "I - don't feel - good."

Hesitantly, I reach forward and rest my hand against the little boy's pale forehead. Instantly, I jerk my hand back in surprise. "Oh... You're burning up, Josh."

Josh lets out a small groan and lets his eyes roll back in his head. "What are we gonna do?"

My hands are still shaking. I don't know how to make them stop. Standing up slowly, I can feel my legs wobbling, as if they're going to give out underneath me. "Well," I begin stammering, swallowing hard, "I - I'm gonna go get something."

"What?"

I wring my hands anxiously. "Medicine or some-thing."

Josh shivers, and my eyes land on a blanket that's sit-ting in a basket in the corner of the living room. I rush over to the basket, grab the blanket, and throw it over Josh, who grabs it eagerly.

"M - maybe you s - should get help," whispers Josh, his teeth chattering.

I can feel my eyes widen in fear. "I can't do that, Josh. We don't need anyone else, even if you're sick. I'll make you better. I promise."

Josh begins coughing violently, and I step back, star-tled. After a moment, he stops, and I look at him one last time before running into my room, grabbing all the money I have, and running out the front door.

The rain is coming down harder than ever, so hard that it's almost blinding, but I don't have time to worry about it. My only goal is to make it to the first drugstore I see and to get as many cold remedies as possible.

* * * * * * * * * *

After what seems like much longer than ten minutes of running, I stumble through the front door of Carlson Drug-store. I quickly realize that I'm one of few customers, thanks to the rain outside. I catch a glance of myself in the reflection of the door and realize how I look; I'm soaking wet, with water dripping from my tangled dark hair. Still, I don't care. All I need to worry about is getting medicine for Josh.

As wet as I am, though, I think to myself, *I can't afford to get sick, too.*

Shaking my head, I step up to the counter and begin talking fast. "I need something for a fever and cough, and chills," I say quickly. "Something that'll work quickly. And maybe something that doesn't taste too bad."

The white-haired man standing at the counter raises his eyebrows, but without saying a word, he turns around and begins browsing through bottles of medicine. After a moment, he hands me one bottle and tells me the price. Thankfully, I have enough money. Handing him the cash, I take the bottle and begin running again, determined to reach Josh - before he gets any worse.

* * * * * * * * * *

"Josh, I'm back," I yell, bursting into the house. Bottle in hand, I rush over to the couch - and stop short when I see Josh's pale, still body.

My palms begin sweating nervously, but I wait a moment. "Josh? Josh, answer me."

No answer. Unable to wait a second longer, I step forward and begin gently shaking the little boy. "Josh, wake up. Answer me. Oh, please, Josh…" I can feel my eyes begin burning, but I refuse to give in. "Josh, come on."

Slowly, very slowly, Josh's green eyes flutter open. "Mark?"

I rub my eyes quickly with the back of my hand. "Yeah, Josh, I'm here. Take this." I pour a bit of medicine out and have Josh drink it. Then, I tuck the blanket around him and sit down on the coffee table, leaning forward. "Go ahead and sleep now. You're gonna be okay. Got it?"

"Uh huh." I watch as Josh drifts back to sleep, his pale face calm and relaxed.

I sit on the table a few more minutes, just to make sure that Josh is okay. Then, I walk to my room, where I collapse on the bed, my head pounding.

Another headache. Perfect. I rub my hands on my jeans and take deep breaths to relieve the pain. I should have known this would happen. Every time I get stressed, my headaches become worse.

I stare out the window and resume watching the rain fall. I've never been so scared before in my life - except for the week following the accident three years ago. This time, it was just as bad - maybe even worse. Because to lose Josh would be one of the worst things that ever happened to me. He's my friend - no, he's like my *brother*. He's the little brother I never had. And I'm never going to let anything happen to him, *ever*.

CHAPTER EIGHTEEN
MARK

My eyes open slowly, and the first thing they land on is the sight of Josh sleeping on the couch, breathing softly. I straighten up in the loveseat where I sat all night, and I rub my neck, trying to stretch it back out. After I calmed down in my room yesterday, I went back out to the living room to look after Josh. I guess I ended up falling asleep.

Quietly, I stand up and walk over to the couch. Pressing my hand gently against Josh's forehead, I breathe a sigh of relief when I realize that his fever has gone down. Comforted by this fact, I walk out of the living room and into the kitchen to get some dry cereal. When I return a couple minutes later, two bowls in hand, I'm greeted by Josh, who is now sitting up and rubbing his eyes.

"Mark?" he says quietly. "What's going on?"

I hand him a bowl and observe his face. Although his temperature went down, he doesn't look well to me. He looks weak.

"Are you hungry?" I ask.

Josh nods. "A little bit. Could I have some water?"

I nod and jog back to the kitchen. Grabbing a glass from the cabinet and filling it with water, I return to the living room and hand it to Josh. A few minutes later, the cereal has been eaten and the water drank, and Josh lays back down. It doesn't take long before his eyes have closed again.

Although I want to always stay by Josh, I'd also like something to do. Curious, I lean forward to pick up *The Count of Monte Cristo*. Staring at the words, I almost smile to myself - because for once, I don't have a headache.

I'm just about to start reading the first page when I notice Josh staring at me. Surprised, I chuckle. "I thought you were asleep."

Josh frowns and cranes his neck to make eye contact with me. "Mark?"

"Hm."

"Are you going to get sick?"

I feel my breath catch in my throat, and I shake my head. "Nah. I'm strong. Even if I did get sick, all you've got is a little cold."

Josh whimpers suddenly, and he begins shivering. I notice that his blanket has come off of him, thanks to the fact that he spent half the night thrashing around on the couch. I drop down at his side and put the blanket back on him, tucking it around his skinny body.

"Mark?"

"Yeah?"

"Am I going to be okay?"

I swallow hard. "Yeah. Of course, you're gonna be okay. What kind of a question is that?"

Josh sighs. "Well - I've gotten sick before."

"So? Everyone gets sick sometimes."

111

"But I got *really* sick. I had to go to the hospital."

I stop suddenly. "You did? W - well, so did I. I mean, everybody goes to the hospital once in a while. I got the flu pretty bad when I was about your age. I came out of it, though."

Josh stares at me. There's a strange look in his innocent, green eyes. "The doctors whispered all the time. I didn't hear everything they said, but I did hear one thing. I heard them say how weak I was. They said I was too weak."

I shudder. I can just imagine the hospital now, with its cold, sterile walls, and whispers of impending death. I've never been good at trusting people - it just never came naturally to me. But of all the people I've met in my life, the ones I trust the least are the ones in white coats who say, "Everything's going to be fine. They'll heal. They'll be okay." Why don't I trust them? Because they lie. They lie every time. And lying is something that I can never do to Josh.

"Maybe you were weak then. But I'm going to do everything I can to make you better. I promise." Every word that comes out of my mouth feels good - because I know that I mean them with all my heart.

Josh nods, and his eyes close slowly, giving me the confidence to believe that maybe, Josh will be okay after all.

* * * * * * * * * *

It's been a week now, and Josh has gotten a little better every day, especially since I picked him up and carried him to our room to get him in his warm bed. But the only thing that worries me is how he hasn't gotten up much to walk around. Every time he walks around a little while, he comes back to his bed as quickly as he can, saying he feels too weak to move much longer.

Every time this happens, I nod and help him back into bed, sure that he'll be up and moving the next day. But I'm beginning to feel less sure of this now. It doesn't take a doctor's diagnosis for me to know that Josh is weak to an unhealthy level.

Besides this, there's also food to worry about. With Josh sick, I've been afraid to leave his side for more than a few minutes, anxiously waiting for the moment that he'll get out of bed and say, "I feel better." This has led to Josh and I being almost completely out of money.

I've desperately wanted to continue working, but there's no way I'm going to leave Josh until I know he'll be okay without me.

Suddenly, I hear a noise, and I watch as Josh rolls over in his bed. Watching him for a moment, I make sure he's okay. Then, I glance out the window and peer into the darkness. It hasn't rained since last week, which means that there's plenty of cars in need of a wash by now.

Laying down hesitantly, I close my heavy eyelids and try to ignore the intense hunger pains in my stomach. I need to work; I know that now. And I need to do it with or without Josh.

* * * * * * * * * *

Two days later, Josh is up and moving around, although very slowly. His pale face is still void of color, and he sleeps more than he used to - but I can tell that he's getting better, which means that it's time for me to go back to work.

After standing in the kitchen for a while to observe the almost-empty cabinets, I turn and walk to mine and Josh's room. Knocking softly on the door, I wait until I hear a small voice call, "Come in."

Walking into the room, I see Josh sitting up in bed, reading. A smile spreads across his freckled face when he sees me. "What's up?"

I bite my lip. "Josh, you're feeling much better, aren't you?"

Josh nods, and I take a deep breath before continuing. "Well - I think it's time that I went back to work."

I expect Josh to be okay with this statement - but his face falls. "You mean 'we,' right? We're going back to work?"

I shake my head slowly. "No, Josh - just me. I - I know you're getting better, but you aren't strong enough to be washing cars all the time. You aren't eating enough - neither of us are. So, I need to go back to work and earn money for us to get food."

Josh tilts his head in confusion. "We still have money. Don't we?"

114

I nod. "Sure - but the kitchen cabinets are empty, and I don't want to use up all our money before earning some more. You know?"

Josh simply stares at me, his face full of disappointment.

I swallow hard, feeling torn apart by Josh's face. "Josh, try to understand -"

"I do understand. I do. Go ahead, Mark. It's alright." Josh puts on a brave face and a smile. "Please, Mark. I'll be okay."

I hesitate, my conscience nagging me. "Are you sure? Ah, maybe I shouldn't leave you alone -"

"No," exclaims Josh, shaking his head. "I'll be alright. I was on my own a long time before you found me, you know. Go on, Mark. We need the money."

I bite my lip. There's a strange sort of emotion in Josh's words - but I can't tell what it is. All I know is, Josh acts much older than he is - and it's sure helpful to me. I give Josh a pat on the shoulder. "Thanks, kid. I'll be back in a couple hours."

* * * * * * * * * *

Walking down the street with a freshly earned pay of six dollars in my pocket, I'm just about ready to fall over from exhaustion and hunger. I'm prepared to head straight to the store, but just as it comes into sight, I realize that I'm walking right past the fast-food restaurant where Josh and I ate a couple weeks ago.

I stop walking suddenly and take a moment to calculate in my head. I have plenty of money for groceries, even if I stop at the restaurant. And it would feel so good to rest for a minute.

Quickly, I make up my mind. I open the door and step inside the restaurant. Walking up to the counter, I realize suddenly that the young man standing there is the same one Josh and I talked to last time. Now, if I could only remember his name…

"Hey, uh, Mike," says the man, taking less than a few seconds to recall my name.

"Hi, um…" I take a moment and snap suddenly. "Steven."

Steven grins. "Yeah." He opens his mouth to say something, but stops quickly and looks around, as if trying to look for someone. Then, he asks, "Where's your partner?"

I bite my lip. "Oh, Tom's at home. He's been sick for a while, so my mom asked me to do some shopping while she takes care of him."

Steven nods, a sympathetic look on his face. "Oh, man. I hope he feels better soon. What kind of a sickness does he have?"

Shrugging, I say, "A cold, I think. He had shivers for a while, but now he's got a cough and is pretty weak."

Steven taps his chin in thought. "Well, what my mom always did was give me some 7UP and saltine crackers. I don't know how, but they always seemed to help. Got me some sugar in the process, too," he laughs.

I crack a small smile on my previously serious face. "Yeah. My mom did - er, does that, too."

I order two hamburgers (one to-go) and sit down at a booth to eat mine. I try to focus on my food, but I can't help thinking about what Steven said. It gets me thinking about my mom. I remember when I would be sick, and she'd give me soup and help me get better. She'd sit by me and read me stories. She'd -

I slam my hand down on the table and rub my forehead. I can't do this to myself. I can't think about the past. Every time I do, it hurts worse than anything else - even more than my headaches. And I hate it.

CHAPTER NINETEEN
TIM

I glance quickly at my watch and squint, holding up my hand to protect my eyes from the bright sun. It's 7 PM, and I've been standing outside of the music store, waiting for Kate. We agreed to meet up in front of the music store, and although this was a fine agreement, I feel a slight twinge of regret over not being able to pick up Kate in a car, the way I should. Kate seemed fine with the suggestion, though, which comforts me a bit.

Turning to observe the store window, I glance inside at all the records. I've just begun looking around when I feel a tap on my shoulder. Whirling around, I find myself face-to-face with Kate, whose big grin seems to take up her whole face.

"Hi," I say.

Her green eyes sparkle as she looks up at me. "Hi." She glances around for a moment, takes a deep breath, and then looks back at me. "Well, are you ready?"

I smile back at her. "Yep."

With that, the two of us begin walking down the sidewalk, side-by-side. Kate's wearing a pretty, warm-looking yellow sweater and jeans today, and this gets me thinking about how much time has passed since I left Green-field. It's October now, and the weather is getting colder every day. Thankfully, I'm still able to pay for my room at the YMCA. I can't imagine how cold I would be if I were sleeping outside instead of getting a room.

After a few minutes of walking and talking together, Kate and I approach the crowded roller rink. "Here we are," exclaims Kate.

I tilt my head up to look at the sign. Then, I look at Kate. "Just so you know - well, I'm not that great at roller skating."

Kate nods for a moment, and then she grins. "Neither am I. I've been practicing, though. Come on - it'll be fun."

Nodding, I take the door and hold it open for her. Then I follow her inside the building. Immediately, I'm almost blinded by the neon-colored lights flashing around the rink. I blink and let my eyes adjust to the lighting. Then, Kate and I walk up to the counter, rent our skates, and head onto the rink.

I hesitate as I begin skating, afraid of falling. I do know how to skate, but I haven't done it in a while. Still, I'm comforted by Kate's presence beside me. She seems hesitant, too, but not a moment has gone by that she hasn't been smiling.

Suddenly, an especially fast skater speeds past us, flying by in a blur. "Woah," I say as Kate and I begin swaying.

Kate laughs as we take a moment to steady ourselves. Continuing, we skate for a little while, focused on staying upright. Then, suddenly, Kate grabs my hand. "Come on. Let's go faster."

I laugh incredulously. "What?"

Kate nods. "We can do it. Let's go."

For a moment, I feel an urge to say no - and then, I throw caution to the wind. Feeling Kate's hand in mine, and feeling a sudden burst of confidence, I begin skating faster, refusing to worry about a thing.

Kate speeds up, too, and we skate together to the tempo of the song playing, which is "Wanna Be Startin' Something" by Michael Jackson. Soon, we've sped up to match the speed of the fastest skaters there, confident and laughing.

Every once in a while, I steal a glance at Kate's face, which is bathed in a neon-yellow glow from the lights dancing across the rink. I've never seen someone so joyful before - someone who seems so happy just to be alive. I love everything about her. Something inside me is telling me that I can't ever let her go. Even though I know that I'll have to say goodbye sometime, though, the way I feel right now makes me wonder if things could be like this forever.

The past couple of weeks I've spent in Davidson have been more fun and - well, normal - for me than anything else I've experienced in years. To top it off, I've never met anyone like Kate before. There's something special about her. In fact, there's something special about this whole town. Something I've never felt before. And all I know is, I wish I could feel it forever.

* * * * * * * * * *

After we've skated for about a half an hour, Kate leads me to the arcade. Still wearing our skates, we browse the arcade games for about a minute - but that's as long as it takes for both of us to find the one game we're both searching for: Pac-Man.

The two of us take turns on the game, trying to focus but unable to stop laughing and glancing at each other. Eventually, we decide to play together. I lay my hand on top of Kate's, and the two of us try working together. It takes a few tries, but eventually, we manage to win.

"Phew," laughs Kate as we release our grip on the yolk. "Good job."

I grin. "That was a workout. Up for a snack?"

Kate nods. "Sure."

The two of us head over to order a couple slices of pizza and some pop. Then, we sit down at a booth with our food and begin talking for a while.

We talk about school, our families, and everything else we can possibly think of. We've been talking for a long time when, suddenly, Kate looks up and widens her eyes in surprise. "Oh, hey, ya'll."

I look up and realize that two people have come and stood at our table. There's a guy who looks to be about my age, with dark hair and a grin. He has his arm around the girl standing next to him, who has glasses and permed blonde hair.

"Uh, Tim," says Kate quickly, "this is Scott Hernandez and Jennifer Connors. Guys, this is Tim. He just moved here a couple weeks ago."

Scott extends his hand towards me, and I shake it. Jennifer gives me a warm smile.

"Hi," I say.

"How're you likin' Davidson, Tim?" asks Scott.

"Oh, it's really nice. Everyone's super welcoming."

Scott nods. Then, after a moment of silence, he says, "Well, we'd better be going. We just wanted to say hi."

Kate begins stammering. "Oh - do you need to rush off so soon?"

Jennifer nods, the look on her face full of regret. "Yeah. My brother needs a ride, so Scott and I are going to pick him up."

Suddenly, I feel as though I've been punched in the gut. At the words "my brother," I feel worried and impatient. I need to leave - *soon*. My bike tire will arrive any day, and then I'll be leaving. And I'll have to say goodbye to Kate.

I don't want to leave Kate. Part of me wishes I'd never even met her, so I wouldn't be in this situation. But my goal this whole time was to find my brother, and that's what I'm going to do.

Kate and I say goodbye to Scott and Jennifer, and I take a moment to muster up some courage. Just as Kate turns towards me to say something, I open my mouth and start talking quickly.

"Kate… I need to tell you something."

Raising her eyebrows, Kate nods. "Okay."

I take a deep breath. "Well - I'm going to be leaving soon. And I might be gone for a long time."

I try to read the look on Kate's face. It appears to be a mix of confusion, hurt, and surprise. "Oh. How long? Where are you going?"

I bite my lip. "I think I mentioned this when I was at your house for dinner, but - well, my parents are taking me on some college visits. We'll be traveling all over. I might not be back in town for a while."

Paying close attention, I notice how Kate seems to gulp when I finish speaking. She avoids my gaze and turns her head to watch all the people skating, their faces full of happiness. We must have looked just like that not more than a half hour ago. Maybe I should've waited to give her the news - but no. She had to find out at some point.

Still, there's an even worse sense of guilt that I'm feeling as I think about the fact that, not only am I disappointing Kate by leaving town so suddenly, but I'm also lying to her as well. I can't tell Kate the truth at this point; I'm sure she'd hate me. But there was no other option. I wanted her to get to know the real me - or at least, the version of me that I see aside from the mess of my life. Besides, it's too dangerous for me to tell the truth. And I told her my real name; that must count for something, right?

Even as I try to reassure myself with these points, Kate's face seems to look sadder and more disappointed. "When are you leaving?" she asks.

I shake my head, answering honestly for once. "I don't know. Any day now, I think."

Kate nods slowly, still refusing to make eye contact with me. Suddenly, words begin flying out of my mouth. "I'm sorry, Kate," I say. "I really am. Maybe I was a jerk to ask you out right before leaving - but I like you a lot. I wanted to get to know you. And - well, I had a lot of fun with you today."

I wait anxiously for Kate to reply. After a few seconds, her green eyes meet mine, and a small smile appears on her face. "I had fun, too."

* * * * * * * * * *

I walk Kate back to her house. It's dark outside now - so dark, in fact, that there's more than a few shining stars visible in the sky.

We don't say much as we walk. I think we're both processing the news that I delivered - news that I wish I'd waited to give. Still, I'm convinced that it was right for me to tell Kate I'm leaving. Although it's hard to process now, we had a good day together, and I think that's all that matters.

Eventually, we reach Kate's house, and I walk her up to the front step. "Well, here we are," I say.

Kate nods slowly. "Yep."

I clear my throat and stand there for a moment, unsure of what to say. Thankfully, Kate helps me out.

"Tim, I've loved getting to know you. I know it's on-ly been two weeks, but - well, it feels like so much longer. I wish you weren't going so soon, but... I can't wait for you to come back."

Suddenly, Kate steps forward and gives me a hug. I wrap my arms around her, and we stand there for a moment. Then, we pull apart, and I stare into Kate's sparkling green eyes one last time. "Bye, Kate." With that, I begin walking down Kate's driveway and then down the sidewalk, my heart heavy.

CHAPTER TWENTY
TIM

It's been a week since the man at the bike shop told me he'd have to order my bike tire. I figure it's about time I check in. So, on a particularly chilly October morning, I wake up with one goal on my mind: to retrieve my bike and head to Charlotte to finally find my brother.

I go through an entire day of work, not wanting to raise suspicion from Mr. Kilmer. Then, I inform him that my family is taking a long trip, and I won't be back for a while. After work, eager to pick up my bike, I find myself practically running all the way to the bike shop. On the way there, I almost run into none other than Kate, who's walking down the street with her parents.

"Hey!" she exclaims when she sees me. "What's up?"

I stop and give her a smile. "Hi. Oh, um, just stopping at the bike shop. What're you doing?"

"Just going to dinner." Kate takes a quick glance at her parents, whose expressions tell me that they're reading her mind. Then she asks, "Do you want to join us?"

I swallow hard. A huge part of me wants to say yes. I love being with Kate - in fact, I love it too much. That's why

126

the words that I force out of my mouth are, "Thanks, but I can't. My parents are expecting me home soon."

Kate nods, a mix of understanding and disappointment on her face. "Alright. Well, I'll see you later."

I nod. "Bye." I give her and her parents a wave, and then I continue running until I reach the bike shop.

Letting the door swing open, I rush inside and am greeted by the same man who I spoke to the last time I came to the shop. "Hi," I say. "I was wondering if my bike's ready yet?"

The man looks down at a piece of paper sitting on the counter and begins scanning it. "Name?"

"Tim Ryder."

After I wait for a moment in silence, the man looks up and shakes his head. "No. Not yet."

I swallow hard and nod, trying not to look too disappointed - but I'm pretty sure I fail at this, because a sympathetic look appears on the man's face.

"I'm sorry, son," he says. "Some of these things take time. It may take another week, at least."

I feel my breath catch in my chest. *A whole other week...*

"Okay. Um... Thank you, sir." I'm about to turn to leave - but, on an impulse, I say, "Is there a way for the bike to be delivered?"

The man nods. "Sure."

I rub my hands together anxiously. "Um... Alright... Do you have a piece of paper I can use? And a pen?"

The man hands me the materials, and I quickly write out Kate's address. Then, I say, "Thank you," and head out the door.

I can't wait any longer to find my brother. In fact, there's no way I'm going to let him wait for me another day. I have enough money to buy myself a bus ticket to Charlotte - and I'm going to do it right now.

* * * * * * * * * *

Sitting at the bus stop with my newly bought one-way ticket in my hand, I can't seem to stop bouncing up and down on the bench, more nervous than I ever thought I'd be. In a matter of minutes, I'll be in Charlotte - and then, I'll be with my brother again.

Suddenly, the bus pulls up, and I go to stand - but I can't. It's hard for me to believe that this is happening. I'm one bus ride away from being with my family... But that also means I'm one bus ride away from leaving the best girl I've ever met.

Quickly, I take a glance over my shoulder towards downtown Davidson. Kate is there right now with her parents, totally unaware that she may never see me again. I told her I was leaving, but I didn't say when. Now, it's too late.

What good would it have done to tell her, though? If I'd told her, then we would've had to say goodbye - and I hate saying goodbye. I've had to say goodbye to too many people in my life, and I'm tired of it. It's better that Kate will never know how I feel. That way, she won't miss me, and she'll eventually forget all about me. Sure, it'll be hard for me to forget about her, but once I'm with Mark again, I'll be so happy and distracted that it won't be long before I stop thinking about my time in Davidson.

I take a deep breath, sling my backpack onto my back, and hop onto the bus - not looking back.

* * * * * * * * * *

The bus ends up making a few stops, and I realize that it'll take a little longer to get to Charlotte than I thought. The whole way there, I can't seem to stop thinking about Mark. I knew I'd find him at some point, but I didn't think it would be this soon. Now, it's happening, and I'm feeling more anxious by the minute.

What if he's different from the way he used to be? After all, it has been three years. He's thirteen now, and he could've changed a lot from the last time I saw him.

On the other hand, I could be faced with the same old Mark. The same old kid with a quick temper who'd make you want to laugh and be mad at him all at the same time. I want things to be exactly the way they were - and somehow, I have a feeling that from now on, things are going to go exactly the way I plan them.

Before I know it, the bus comes to a final halt, and the driver announces, "Charlotte, North Carolina."

Excitedly, I stand up immediately and walk off the bus. When I step off, I feel as though I've been hit in the face full force, a thousand memories flooding my brain.

I haven't been in the city for over three years, but I never expected it'd feel this strange to be back.

A chill appears in the air, and I shiver inside my jacket. It's late, but I don't want to wait a second longer to find Mark. So, I begin walking down the street, hoping that my navigational skills will be enough to help me locate his foster home. If I can find it, then I'll be with Mark again in less than an hour. I'll finally be with my brother again.

As I walk, I think about all the things I'd like to do with Mark. I wish we could walk around Charlotte and take in all the sights that we used to see when we were kids. I wish we could stop by our old school. I wish we could say hello to our old friends. Part of me even wishes we could visit our old apartment. But all these wishes are just that - wishes. They'll never come true. Because as soon as I find Mark, the two of us are going to have to leave the city - and even the state. We can't stick around here anymore. We'll be on the run, and we won't be able to stop for a while. But I don't think Mark will care. All that matters is that we're together again.

CHAPTER TWENTY-ONE
MARK

When it comes to working, some days are better than others. For me, today is a super bad day.

It started like any other day that I've had for the past many weeks. I got out of bed, said goodbye to Josh, and went out to look for cars to wash. I knocked on the first door I saw and was turned down. Then, I tried again, on the next door. I had to knock on at least ten different doors before finally, I got a "yes."

Now, I'm washing the shiny yellow car in front of me as a bunch of dark clouds begin to roll into the sky. My back begins to hurt, and I stand up straight to stretch it out. I close my eyes for half a second - and am greeted by a gigantic wet drop hitting my forehead.

I open my eyes and reach up to wipe off my forehead, expecting to see a light drizzle of rain - but it isn't light. In fact, it's pouring.

Groaning, I give the car one last swipe with my rag and rush up to the front door of the small, brick house, knocking quickly. The door opens to reveal the man I spoke to about forty-five minutes ago. At first, there's a smile on his face, but it quickly changes to a look of realization when he sees the hard rain beginning to fall.

"I'm all finished, sir," I say breathlessly. "I just thought you should know it might be a good idea to get the car inside your garage."

The man nods, his glasses sliding down his nose. He pushes them back up and looks at me with his caramel-colored eyes. "Yes, I'll do that. Thanks. Give me one minute."

I wait a moment before the man returns with two dollars. "Here's your pay."

I nod. "Thank you."

With that, I begin walking down the street, my hands stuffed in my pockets. I don't know what to do now; I can't wash any more cars, but I certainly can't go back to the cabin and face Josh with a mere two dollars in my hand. Every day, when I return from working, Josh asks me to tell him about my day. He says he likes me to tell stories. He likes to know what life is like outside the cabin these days. Without fail, I tell him everything he wants to know, knowing that maybe, if I do what he wants, then he'll keep doing what I want: resting and staying safe at the cabin.

If I go back to the cabin now, all I'll have to tell Josh about is how I was rejected ten times, got one job, and had to finish quickly because it started raining. I feel the two one-dollar bills sitting in my pocket and wish they would magically multiply in my hand. Our money supply is filling quickly, thanks to the fact that I've been working every day - but having a day like this makes me feel too discouraged to do it anymore.

Walking by the park where Josh and I stopped many weeks ago, I look far into the distance and can almost see Josh sitting warmly in the cabin, the rain pouring around him. Then, I look to the left; nearby sits downtown Andersonville, beckoning to me with its warm restaurants and smiling people. The cabin is much further than downtown - so I make a quick decision. I'll wait somewhere downtown until the rain stops falling. Then, I'll head back to the cabin - and maybe I'll have something else to tell Josh about.

* * * * * * * * * *

Stepping inside Andersonville Diner, I'm greeted by its now-familiar smell (a combination of fries, grease, and smoke). I expect to see the face of Steven, and I do - but the first thing I notice about it is how flushed it is.

I watch from a distance as Steven rushes around the restaurant, yelling things like "Two hamburgers, hold the tomato." Although I usually see him working at the counter, he seems to be everywhere at once today, shouting orders and wiping sweat from his brow.

I take my place in line behind ten other people and watch as Steven works. I expect the line to move quickly, but it doesn't. Steven looks more flustered than I've ever seen him before - and I've made plenty of stops at the restaurant these past few weeks.

After about five minutes, I've reached the front of the line. I open my mouth to say hello to Steven, but he doesn't even make eye contact with me. Instead, he mechanically asks, "Hi, what can I get you today?"

I tilt my head and laugh. "Steven? It's me. M - Mike."

Steven looks up suddenly and laughs sheepishly. He leans forward and lowers his voice, which loses its mechanical tone. "Oh, hey, Mike. Geesh, I didn't even know it was you. Man, it's been so busy today, I can't even begin to -"

"Hey, Steven, we need you back here!" a young red-haired guy hollers from the kitchen.

Steven rubs his face with his hand and looks over his shoulder. "Ya'll just hang tight without me a sec, alright?"

He turns back to me and shakes his head, an incredulous look on his face. "I'm tellin' ya, Mike, all these people we've got working here - well, they're great, but... There's just not enough of 'em."

I take a quick look at the kitchen. There are only three other workers besides Steven where there should be five or six.

"Well," I say, stuffing my hands in my pockets, "it seems to me you need more help around here. Only... I remember you saying a while back that you weren't hiring."

Steven sighs, a defeated look on his face. "Well, yeah, that's right. I wasn't... Not then. But I had a couple people quit. One moved, and the other got a different job.

We're more shorthanded now than we've ever been. I guess I'd better find some people soon."

I fold my arms across my chest and stand up as straight as I can. "Well... How about me?"

Steven is quiet for what seems like much more than a minute. For a moment, I wonder if there's a chance that Steven will say no - so I'm surprised when a smile appears on his face, and he nods eagerly.

"Yeah," he exclaims. "Yeah, that'd be great. How old are you again, Mike?"

"Thirteen," I say, my voice quiet. "B - but almost fourteen! My birthday's real soon."

Steven nods, and I feel the need to continue talking. "I'm a hard worker. I've been washing lots of cars lately, just to save up some money. I know how to get things done."

Steven continues nodding. "Yeah, I'm sure you do. That settles it, then - you've got the job."

I grin, and I can feel my eyes light up. I stick out my hand and give Steven's a shake. "Aw, thanks, Steven. You won't regret this."

Steven grins back at me, and he stands up straight. "So - what'll you have?"

I scan the menu for a moment. Excitedly, on a whim, I exclaim, "A vanilla shake."

Nodding, Steven calls my order over his shoulder. Then, with a wink, he says, "Take a seat, employee."

CHAPTER TWENTY-TWO
MARK

I smooth out my freshly pressed shirt and nervously brush my hair out of my face. I've just changed into my new uniform, and now I've been sitting at a booth in the restaurant, waiting for Steven to give me a quick "orientation." He told me that, as he's the assistant manager, it's his job to give me a quick run-down of how the restaurant operates, and then I'd start working. He's setting things up in the kitchen right now - and the more time that goes on, the more terrified I am.

I've never had a real job before. What if I screw things up so bad that Steven has to fire me? What if I mess up someone's order? What if -

"Hey, Mike," says Steven, walking over.

I stand up quickly and immediately stop my terrible nervous habit of picking at my fingernails. "Hi."

"Well, let's see if I can get you introduced to some people around here, and then I'll give you a little bit of a tour."

I follow Steven to the kitchen and am met by three smiling teenagers. Two are girls, and one is a guy. Steven takes a moment to introduce me to each one. "This is Tracy," he says, pointing to the first girl. As I stare at the tall, blonde, blue-eyed girl who can't be more than sixteen, I feel my heart skip a beat as we make eye contact.

"Hey," she says, a hint of laughter playing along her lips.

I realize that I may be displaying my emotions on my face, and I quickly give her a casual nod. "Hi."

Steven moves on to the next girl. "This is Ashley."

I take in this girl for a moment. Her permed brown hair is so long, it's impressive; even in a ponytail, it reaches all the way down her back. This girl is a bit shorter than the other, and a bit older; I'm guessing she's around nineteen years old.

Ashley greets me, and then Steven introduces me to the guy, who happens to be attached to Ashley's hip. "And this is Davey."

Davey, a skinny, red-haired guy who's about an inch taller than Ashley but looks to be her age, extends his free hand and gives mine a shake. "Welcome to the team, Mike."

I shake his hand firmly and give him a smile. "Thanks."

Steven claps me on the shoulder and begins leading me around the kitchen. "Well, now that you've met every-body, I can start showing you the ropes. This here's the drive-thru window. Usually, Tracy handles that, but we rotate sometimes."

I nod, and Steven leads me over to the front counter. "This is where you'll spend most of your time. I usually handle the front counter, but now that we've got you to help us out, you'll be taking it over."

I open my mouth to say something, but Steven reads my mind and says, "Don't worry. I'm about to teach you everything you'll need to know."

Steven then proceeds to explain how I should take orders and pass them onto the kitchen. To my surprise, this only takes ten minutes, and I understand everything perfectly. As soon as he finishes explaining, he asks, "Do you understand all that?"

I nod, and I can see a hint of surprise flash across Steven's face. "Alright," he says, "let's test you out, then."

He exits from behind the counter and enters the line, pretending to be a customer. I stand there for a moment, too nervous to know what to say. Then, Steven clears his throat, and I snap into action.

"Hello," I say, "what can I get you today?"

Steven taps his chin in mock thought. "Hmm... I think I'll have a cheeseburger, no pickles, a side of fries, and a root beer."

Concentrating now, I nod, pass the order along, and pretend to perform a transaction. Once I've finished, Steven grins and gives me a nod of approval. "Yeah, you're a natural. You'll do just fine."

* * * * * * * * * *

Two hours later, it's noon - the diner's busiest time of day, according to Steven. I can tell that he's right, because a long line forms just as soon as the clock changes to twelve.

I spend the next hour working quickly, concentrating hard and trying not to become flustered. Occasionally, Steven comes over and helps me when things become too busy. He seems so calm today, as if merely having one new presence in the kitchen is enough.

Once the clock turns to 1 PM, the line thins out, and Steven appears beside me to help me finish. When the last customer finishes ordering, Steven taps me on the shoulder, and I turn around.

"Go ahead and take your lunch break now," he says. "We haven't been able to handle this many customers so quickly in a long time. You're doin' real good."

I push my dark brown hair out of my eyes and grin. "Thanks."

"Go sit down at a table, and I'll bring you something. How's a burger sound?"

"Sounds good to me."

It's only when I sit down at the table that I realize how tired I am. I've been working non-stop since 10:30 AM, and I haven't had one moment to myself.

It only takes a minute before Steven arrives at my table, carrying my food. "Here you go."

I smile. "Thanks, Steven."

Suddenly, I notice that Steven is holding something under his arm. "What's that?"

Steven glances down at his arm in surprise, as if he forgot what he was holding there. Taking it, he holds it out to me for a moment. "Oh, just a book. Things seem calm enough for me to take my break after yours, so I was just gonna do some reading."

I squint. The book is called *A Tale of Two Cities*. It looks long to me - too long. "You like reading?"

Steven nods. "Yeah. Passes the time - or, at least, the little free time I have when I'm not workin'."

I take one last look at the book. The cover looks so familiar to me that I'm sure I've seen it somewhere before - maybe in a bookstore or something like that.

"Well - enjoy your break, Mike," says Steven as he walks away.

I nod. "Thanks."

Glancing out the window, I look through the trees in the distance and am almost able to see Josh at the cabin, waiting for me. I told him about my job, but I never expected it to be this great. I'll be coming home with plenty of money to last us a long time, and Josh doesn't even have to work. He can do whatever he wants at the cabin, just like any other kid - and I can keep working and support him, like the older brother I'm trying to be to him. I can't wait to tell him about the day; he's sure to love hearing about it.

* * * * * * * * *

Opening the front door of the cabin, I holler, "Josh, I'm home."

There's no need for Josh to reply, because the second I step into the living room, I see him sitting on the couch, reading. He looks up at me and gives me a small smile - but I sense a strange hint of some emotion in it. Something like… sadness.

"Hey," I say, sitting down next to him. "What's goin' on?"

Josh shrugs and looks back down at his book. "Nothing. Nice shirt."

I laugh. "Do anything today?"

"No."

I take a deep breath and let my smile melt. Something's wrong - I can tell. Josh has never acted like this before.

"Are you hungry?"

Josh shrugs again, and I reveal the paper bag that I've been hiding behind my back. "Brought you some food from the restaurant."

I hold the bag out to Josh, and he takes it - but nothing changes about the look on his face. "Thanks."

Confused and frustrated, I cross my arms and frown. "Josh, what's up? You're acting - well, weird."

Josh shrugs. He's silent for a moment. I stare at my hands, wondering what to say next. Suddenly, I hear Josh say, "I'm leaving."

My head snaps up, and I stare at the little boy, my heart racing. "What?"

Josh bites his lip. "I'm leaving. I have to."

"B - but - why?"

Josh hesitates, and I groan in frustration. "Josh, come on. What're you talkin' about?"

"I have to leave because - because you're gone all the time." The words are flying out of Josh's mouth now. "You leave me at the house, all alone, and I don't have anything better to do than read. I know I'm just a kid, and you have to leave me here while you work - but I'm not sick anymore. I may have been pretty weak before, but I'm not anymore. You're just never around, and I can't even help you work anymore, so... I think it'd be better if I leave."

I gape at the little boy. His green eyes are wide, and his words passionate. I can tell that he means what he's saying - and I hate the way the words pierce me. I hate the words because I know that they're true. Everything Josh is saying is true - but I've just been too busy to realize it on my own.

Panicking, I start talking fast. "Josh, I'm - I'm really sorry. I've just been so busy working, and you were sick, so I wanted you to rest, and by the time you were better, I got that new job at the restaurant."

Josh shrugs. "It's fine. I understand."

"No, no, you don't. Josh, sometimes I'm busy, but that's only because I'm trying to earn enough money to take care of both of us. I want you to be happy." I expect some sort of change in Josh's expression to tell me that he's beginning to believe my words - but he continues staring at his book, refusing to make eye contact with me.

I swallow hard. I'm not good at saying exactly what I feel... but I might need to do just that right now in order to keep Josh with me. "Josh," I say slowly, "I really care about you. You're like - like my little brother. And I just wanted to protect you by keeping you here. But - I should've asked you what you wanted. I'm sorry."

Finally, a small hint of a smile creeps onto Josh's face - and to my surprise, he says, "I forgive you, Mark."

Allowing myself to breathe again, I grin and ruffle Josh's red hair. "Thanks, kid. Now - how about you come with me to work tomorrow? I'll ask Steven if it's alright."

Josh nods enthusiastically - and just like that, he's back to his old self. "Okay."

CHAPTER TWENTY-THREE
TIM

I've been walking through Charlotte for half an hour. At this point, I begin to wonder if I even know where I'm going. No part of me wants to admit that I may need help getting around the city; it would be like admitting that I'm not the Tim Ryder I used to be. But if I want to find my brother, then I might just have to do it.

My eyes land on a middle-aged man who's sitting on a bench and reading a newspaper. I turn to him and begin talking quickly. "Uh, sir? Can you point me to the Bentwood Foster Home?"

The man turns to me and says, "Just keep walking straight, and then take a left. It's right there." He points straight ahead of me.

I give him a smile. "Thank you."

I'm so excited that I would run all the way down the street if I had the energy. But I'm exhausted, so I settle for walking as fast as I can. *Keep walking straight. Take a left.*

I reach the end of the street. I take a left. I walk a few steps and then look at the sign on the door to my left. It says, "Bentwood Foster Home."

Everything still feels like a dream. Like I fell asleep when I was fourteen years old and still haven't woken up.

But I know that this is all real - and I know that in just a few minutes, I'm going to see my little brother again.

I watch everything happen in slow motion. I reach out and knock on the door. It's opened by a middle-aged woman with blonde hair.

"Hello," she says. "Can I help you?"

I wring my hands together anxiously. *Breathe, Ryder. Breathe.*

"Uh, yes. I'm looking for someone, and I think he's here."

"A child?"

"Yes."

The woman opens the door wider, and I step inside. Standing in the foyer, I see that I'm surrounded by many doors and many hallways. My heart leaps as I realize that my brother could be through one of those doors.

"Now," says the woman, "who are you looking for?"

"A kid. Well - I guess he's not really a kid any-more... He's thirteen. His name is Mark."

The woman raises her eyebrows. "Mark Ryder?"

I feel my breath catch in my throat at the sound of his name. I haven't heard anyone say it in a long time. "Yes!" I exclaim, my face lighting up. "Can I see him?"

"Who are you?"

I mechanically begin to tell the lie that I made up as I walked to the foster home. Standing a little taller, I say, "My name's Andrew Baxter. I'm a family friend."

The woman looks closely at me. Then, she shakes her head. "I'm sorry. You can't see him."

"Why not?"

The woman hesitates. "Well, because… He's gone."

I can feel my face go deathly white. "What? What do you mean?"

"He ran away about two months ago, in the middle of the night."

Just like that, I can feel myself begin to sway. I turn and lean onto the wall for support. The woman is talking to me, but I don't hear her. The only thing that I can think about right now is my brother, all alone somewhere without anyone looking out for him. It's almost as bad as if he were dead - *almost*.

"Do you need any help?" I can hear the woman ask me.

I shake my head and try to compose myself. "N - no. I'm okay. But - do you have any idea where he is?"

"No. I'm very sorry."

I try to stand up straight and make eye contact with the woman. I can feel my eyes begin to burn, and I rub them quickly, trying to conceal my emotions. "Well - is anything being done to find him? I mean - were the police notified?"

"Oh, of course," says the woman, nodding. "They were notified immediately. They're actively looking, and his picture is in many missing persons ads, and -"

"Missing persons ads?" I whisper, beginning to lose my temper. "They think that missing persons ads will help find him? How in the heck do they think -"

"Mr. Baxter, I assure you, the police are doing everything they can. No one feels more regret about the situation than I, but there simply isn't anything more we can do than wait. The police know what they're doing."

I've never felt so angry and confused in my entire life. Shaking my head, I turn quickly and begin walking towards the door. Before I exit, however, I say, "I've waited too long to just be told to wait even more. I'm done waiting." With that, I tear through the front door, pulling it shut behind me.

* * * * * * * * * *

I walk through the streets of Charlotte half the night, simply wandering, not quite sure where I am. My mind is hazy, and as I walk through the city which used to be so familiar to me, my memories fly through my head like a blur.

Pretty soon, I've become too tired to walk, and I settle down on a park bench for the remainder of the night - but I don't sleep. I can't stop thinking about Mark. All I can see is his face flashing through my mind. It's the ten-year-old version of himself - the last one I saw. I wish I could imagine his face now, but I can't. Now, I'm not sure if I ever will.

Before I know it, I've sat up almost all night, and the sun is beginning to rise. Standing up slowly, I begin walking again. I don't know how long I walk, but by the time I decide to glance at my watch, it says that it's around 9 AM.

I don't know where I'm going, but somehow, I end up back at Bentwood Foster Home. To my surprise, the place seems busy today, with noise and music pouring out of the open windows and kids running around outside. I step close to the building and watch the scene playing out before me.

I'm so lost in my own world that I don't notice a tall, blond-haired kid approaching me. "Hey," he says.

I blink to escape my daze, and I look at the boy. "Oh. Hi."

The boy squints at me, a strange look on his face. Then, suddenly, he says, "You look like Mark."

My eyes widen, and I stare at the boy, giving him my full attention. "You - you know Mark?"

The boy nods. "Yeah. How do you know him?"

I hesitate before answering, "I'm Tim Ryder. His brother."

The boy looks closely at me. "Yeah. I can tell."

I raise my eyebrows. No one has ever told me that Mark and I look alike before. People always said that I looked the most like our mom, and Mark like our dad.

"What's your name?" I ask.

"Ben Robinson."

"And - you knew Mark before he ran away? Did you know him well?"

Ben nods slowly, as if trying to think of what to say. "Pretty well. Ah, well... You know how Mark is. It took a while for us to become friends - if you could call us that."

"What? Why?" I ask in confusion.

Ben crosses his arms against his chest. "Well... He was quiet. He hardly ever said anything to anybody, and when he did, it was pretty sarcastic. Honestly, he's probably the most untrusting kid I've ever known."

I swallow hard. "What else?" I suddenly feel desperate to learn everything I can about the kid who I no longer know.

"He always felt shut up here - trapped. I could tell he was always longing for something else - something *more*, you know? He'd had plenty of foster families take him in, but I don't think he ever made much of an effort to make them like him. I know that because he never lasted long with any family, and he always returned after a month or so - sometimes less."

The pain I've had in my stomach since last night is beginning to grow as I hear Ben talk about Mark. It sounds like Ben knows Mark better than I ever did - and it scares me. I thought that by this time today, things would be the way they were three years ago... But they couldn't be more different.

"Do you know where he was going when he ran away?" I ask.

Ben shakes his head, a look of regret on his face. "No. I didn't really know he was going to do it until it happened. I'm sorry."

I nod slowly. Then, Ben asks, "I was wondering… Where have you been? I mean, what happened to you and Mark?"

I feel my fists clench and unclench as I recall the most painful memories from my life. "We were separated. I haven't seen Mark in three years."

The look on Ben's face turns to a mix of sadness and pity. "I'm sorry. I wish I could help you. I just don't know where he went. All I know is, I'm sure he wanted to get as far away from here as possible."

I nod. "Yeah. Well - thanks."

Ben nods. "Sure. I really hope you find him."

"Me too."

CHAPTER TWENTY-FOUR
TIM

After my talk with Ben, I walked through Charlotte for a long time, stopping by all the familiar parks and apartments. I even saw my old elementary school and middle school. But the thing I'm least prepared to see is the last one I end up passing by.

I don't realize I'm standing in front of my family's old apartment for a while. I just get the sense that I'm somewhere very familiar. Then, it hits me - and my entire childhood flashes through my mind.

As I stare up at the apartment, I can almost see Mark's ten-year-old face peering out to look down at me. I can almost hear his little voice echoing through the air. Part of me can even hear my parents' voices - although they're much fainter and stranger to me. Like soft whispers, their voices float gently down to me. For a moment, I enjoy them. Then, suddenly, the voices change. They become angry, loud, and upset. And the look on Mark's innocent, happy face transforms to a look of disappointment... and even hatred.

Shuddering, I jog down the dimly lit street, not stopping until I'm far away from the old apartment. There are too many memories there. And although I try to move on from them now, I'm filled with regret over all the hardship that Mark has gone through in his life. I could've saved him from some of that - and I failed. *I failed.* I made a promise I couldn't keep, and Mark was the one who paid for it. He must hate me. He must really hate me.

Walking through a park, I spot a bench to sit down on. As I sit, a couple of birds on a nearby tree branch take flight. They look so happy - so free. It pains me to think that Mark felt trapped for so long, and the only reason he ran away was to find some freedom of his own. I could've given him that freedom years ago if I'd had the means to. I thought I had to wait until I was older, just to make sure I'd be able to support the two of us. Now, I know that I waited much too long - and I'm too late.

Shivering, I fold my arms across my chest and try to warm up. The temperature can't be more than fifty degrees - a telltale sign that it's almost November. I shiver as I think of Mark somewhere, out in the cold, completely unaware that I've been looking for him.

I lean back on the bench and cover my face with my hands. I've never been so ashamed of myself in my life. Not only does Mark probably hate me, but now *I* hate myself, too.

Staring up at the dark clouds that are beginning to roll in, I realize something. With no money and no means of finding my brother, the only option I have is to settle down someplace until an opportunity to find Mark presents itself. Greenfield is out of the question, and Charlotte is more unfamiliar and haunting to me than ever. Which means... My only other option, besides striking out to a new place, is to go back to Davidson.

If I do, I can ask Mr. Kilmer for my job back. I'll be able to settle back into my life in Davidson while I do as much as I can to try to find Mark. I may not succeed right away... But at least I'll be with people I know while I have to wait.

Standing up slowly, I begin walking back in the direction I came. I don't have any money left, which means I'll have to walk all the way back to Davidson. It'll take a long time, but at least I'll be with Kate by the end of it.

This isn't the thought that continues to run through my mind, though. Instead, it's the thought of Mark, all alone someplace. He's almost fourteen - but that's still too young for him to be by himself. He should be with me, and the fact that he isn't is all my fault.

* * * * * * * * * *

Since it's already late by the time I've made the decision to go back to Davidson, I spend the night sitting in the doorway of my old apartment, the shadows hiding me from view until the sun comes up. The next step is to get up and begin traveling.

I don't know how long I walk before I'm out of the city, but it seems like forever. Now, I'm walking through what I can tell is a small, suburban town. Many of the houses are quiet and appear to be empty. I don't know why until I pass by a little, white-painted church and realize that it's Sunday morning.

When my family used to go to church, it was usually for Easter, Christmas, and an occasional Sunday - and those were few and far between. By now, it's been years since I've entered one.

Now, for reasons I don't understand, my feet seem to be taking me towards the church instead of towards Davidson. About thirty cars are parked outside the building. I'm surprised that so many people can fit inside such a small space.

I keep walking until I've reached the front door of the church. I can hear singing and the shuffling of feet; the church must be packed to the rafters. I highly doubt that there's room for me, but almost unconsciously, I find myself opening the door and walking inside.

Only a few people bother to turn around to look at me. I just give them a small, forced smile and find a seat in the back of the church.

A minute later, the current hymn ends, and "Amazing Grace" begins. I almost sigh in relief at the somewhat-familiar tune. I don't sing along with the rest of the congregation; I simply listen and take in my surroundings.

Half the people in the church are adults, while a few are young kids and even fewer are teenagers. Most of the people, dressed in Sunday dresses and dress shirts, look like they know what they're doing here. After a couple more minutes, the hymn ends, and everyone sits down. The pastor, a tall man with graying brown hair, walks up to the pulpit, and the entire room goes quiet immediately. Even the four little girls at the back of the room who were whispering together before are now silent.

I can feel my palms begin to sweat. *What am I doing here? Why am I wasting my time? I know what the pastor's about to say. I know he'll tell the same stories and talk about how blessed people are. I've heard it all before, and none of it has helped me get through life. None of it has helped me find Mark. So why am I here?*

Although I have an urge to bolt, the pastor begins to speak, obligating me to stay where I am. I don't expect to hear much - but I can't leave now. I don't have any other choice.

CHAPTER TWENTY-FIVE
MARK

"Hey, guys!" exclaims Steven as Josh and I enter the restaurant. "Got any good books for me today, Tom?"

It's been over a week since I first brought Josh into the restaurant in the hopes that he could stay there while I worked. Now, I've gotten to know all the other workers better, and so has he. In fact, he and Steven have bonded over their mutual love of reading. Every day, Steven and Josh have exchanged book recommendations and taken the time to talk.

I've never thought I was much good at talking to kids, but I figured I was getting better since I met Josh. Compared to Steven, though, I feel like I have no idea what I'm doing. Steven acts as though he's used to little kids. He knows how to talk to Josh in just the right way. At first, he seemed a bit surprised at Josh's excitement and eagerness to read at such a young age. Then, he couldn't get enough of it. He peppered Josh with questions about all his favorite books - which was a relief to me, since he was asking the easiest questions Josh could answer, instead of personal ones.

"Yeah," exclaims Josh, rushing up to the counter and receiving a high-five from Steven. "I read this great book yesterday called *To Kill a Mockingbird*. It's one of the classics."

"Ah," says Steven, "I've read that one before. It was years ago, though, when I was still in school. I wasn't much into reading then. Maybe I should re-read it."

Josh nods, and Steven's eyes light up as he extends his arm towards the little boy. A book is in his hand. It takes me no time at all to realize that it's the very same book he was reading on my first day of work: *A Tale of Two Cities*.

Again, the cover strikes me as familiar, but I only observe it from afar as Steven hands it to Josh. "Wow," breathes Josh as his big green eyes take in the cover. "Thanks, Steven!"

Steven grins and ruffles Josh's hair. "Sure."

"Wow. That one always sounded kind of complicated to me," I say, watching Josh flip through the book.

Steven shakes his head. "You act like you don't know your brother. Tom is advanced for his age - that much is clear. I'll give him any books he thinks he can handle. Isn't that right, Tom?"

Josh nods eagerly. "Yeah. Besides, Ma - *Mike*, I'll be eight in December. That's pretty old."

"Oh," I say, trying to hide the smirk creeping across my face.

Steven laughs and gives Josh a pat on the shoulder. "Go ahead and start reading. Mike's going to be extra busy today."

157

Josh nods and runs over to a booth. I look at Steven, a questioning look on my face. "Why am I gonna be extra busy today?"

"Well, it's Saturday," answers Steven as we walk into the kitchen.

"So? We're always busy on Saturdays," I laugh. "What's different about today?"

Steven bites his lip. "Ashley's got the flu. She's one of our best workers, so we're gonna be shorthanded."

I shrug. "Well, I don't think it should be a problem. I mean, you've got me now, don't you?"

"Sure, and you're doing great," says Steven. "But you didn't let me finish. Davey's sick, too. So that's *two* people gone, on a Saturday of all days. It'll be difficult to handle that. Besides, I'm not sure it's such a coincidence that they're *both* sick - you get what I'm sayin'?"

Just like that, it hits me. Shaking my head and laughing, I say, "Why don't we swing by one of their houses and investigate?"

Steven laughs and shakes his head. "Nah. As entertaining as that would be, I'm not in the mood to stand there and listen to Davey's horrible 'sick' voice." He uses his fingers to create air quotes around the word 'sick.' "Besides, they're good kids, and they've never pulled a stunt like that before - so I'm willing to give them the benefit of the doubt."

I shrug. "I guess they're pretty lucky to have such a laid-back boss, then."

Steven shrugs as he approaches the other side of the counter and slides his newest book over to a hidden corner to make way for customers. "Well, I never thought I'd be an assistant manager, that's for sure. I didn't join the restaurant business with high hopes or anything like that - I just needed a job."

I nod. "Yeah. Me too."

Suddenly, Steven lets out a gasp of realization. He stops pushing items aside on the counter and picks up a coloring book and a box of crayons. "Almost forgot!" Without explaining, he exits the kitchen and walks over to Josh, who takes a moment to look up from his book.

I can't hear what's said, but I watch as Steven hands the coloring book and crayons to Josh, who accepts them with a big grin on his freckled face. Then, Steven returns, wearing a satisfied look.

Unable to wait any longer, I ask suddenly, "Steven, how'd you get to be so good with kids?"

Steven laughs, and a few strands of dark hair fall in his eyes. "Aw, I'm not good at it. It's just instinct, right?"

I shake my head and frown. "No, it can't be. I mean, I'm not good with kids at all."

Steven leans against the wall and crosses his arms against his chest. "I don't believe that for a second. After all, you've got Tom for a brother, don't you?"

"Yeah."

"And are you the oldest?"

"Mhm."

"So… You've been an older brother for, what, almost eight years? That's plenty of time to learn how to talk to kids."

I shake my head, wishing there was some way for me to explain to Steven that I'm actually the youngest, and Josh isn't my brother - but this isn't the time for me to start telling the truth. So, I simply say, "I don't know. I guess it just doesn't come that easy to me."

Steven smiles sympathetically. "Well, I guess I've probably just had more practice. I grew up with younger brothers in a big family, so I had to learn how to be an older brother pretty fast."

I nod, and Steven glances up at the clock hanging on the wall. "Oh," he exclaims, "it's showtime." Walking over to the front window, he changes the sign in the window to "OPEN." Then, he rushes back to the kitchen, ready for another day of work.

Customers begin pouring in quickly, keeping me busy all day - and as the day goes on, my head begins to pound. *Not now,* I groan inwardly. *Not today.* Luckily, the pain subsides quickly - but the thought of it lingers as I work, waiting nervously for another headache to strike.

CHAPTER TWENTY-SIX
MARK

I wake up on November 22nd with the same expectations as always. Every day, I get up, go to work, and go home. That's the way it's been for a long time now, and I'm used to it. But, as I blink and let my eyes adjust to the light flooding into my room, I remember something: Today is my fourteenth birthday.

I used to get so excited about my birthday. Most years, I would come home from school to find that my mom had baked a cake. My favorite kind was chocolate fudge, and in the ten birthdays that I got to spend with my family, my mom never forgot to make that cake. It didn't matter whether she was busy, sick, or tired - she always tried to make my birthday special.

I sit up in bed and shiver - partly from the cold weather, and partly because now, I'm thinking about the three birthdays I had to spend at various foster homes or with foster families. They all knew my birthday, and some even made a cake - but no one could ever make me feel special the way my mom did. And whenever they tried, it just made me hurt worse.

Looking over at the other side of the bedroom, my eyes land on Josh. He looks so warm and comfortable in his bed - and so peaceful. I hate to wake him, but every day, he insists on joining me at work, even if it means losing some sleep.

Getting up, I walk over to Josh's bed and begin shaking him gently. "Josh. Time to wake up. I've gotta get to work."

Josh's eyes begin fluttering, and he opens one halfway to look at me. "Okay," he mumbles, rolling over in bed.

I crack a smile and head out of the room. Walking into the bathroom, I splash some water on my face to wake myself up. Then, I stare at myself in the mirror for a moment, observing myself.

When I was a kid, I would look at myself in the mirror every morning and observe myself thoroughly, just to see if I looked any different or any taller. Now, as I take in my dark brown hair and sharp, bluish-green eyes, I don't notice any difference from yesterday to today - but what I do know is that I don't look anything like I did four years ago.

Taking a deep breath, I begin combing my hair. I didn't say much to Josh about today being my birthday; I only mentioned it once, a couple weeks ago. I doubt he'll remember, which means that my birthday won't be acknowledged by anyone. Today will be a day like any other. That's mostly fine by me - but part of me wishes that things were the way they used to be, just so that for one day out of the year, I could feel noticed.

* * * * * * * * * *

Walking to the restaurant, Josh is mostly quiet, his big, green eyes simply taking in his surroundings. He seems extra tired today, but I know he'll pep up with some food (and maybe a little coffee, as Steven let him try some one time, and he didn't entirely hate it).

In his hand, Josh is carrying a new book to bring to Steven. It's the one he started reading a while ago, called *The Count of Monte Cristo*. Josh just recently finished reading it, and he hasn't been able to stop talking about it. I'm not much for reading, but I try to pay attention to Josh's explanation of the plot as much as I can.

It doesn't take long before we've reached the restaurant. We're just about to open the door when I stop walking and take a glance through the window. Steven is already wearing a look of anticipation on his face - a look that only shows up on Saturdays.

"Mark? Are you coming?" asks Josh, who's already holding the door open.

I nod and hold a finger to my lips. "Yeah. Remember, it's *Mike* here."

Josh's eyes widen in realization, and he nods quickly. "Oh. Yeah. Come on, Mike."

I give Josh a grin and follow him inside the restaurant. As soon as we step through the door, Steven looks up and smiles. "Hey, ya'll. What have you got there, Tom?"

Josh rushes forward and hands him the book. "It's a really good one!"

Steven's eyes widen, and he chuckles as he turns the book over, obviously marveling at the length. "And it looks long… You read this, Tom?"

Josh nods, and I see a look of pride flash across his face. "Yeah. It's not very difficult - I think you'll like it."

Steven grins and gives Josh a pat on the shoulder. "I'm sure I will." Then, he turns to me. "Well, how're you feelin', Mike? Ready for today?"

I shrug. "I think so. Have we got everybody in the kitchen today?"

Nodding, Steven gives me a satisfied expression and motions towards Ashley and Davey, who are practically attached at the hip as they stand over the sink together. "Yeah, thank goodness. Even though I know we can handle things without them, it sure makes it a lot easier to have everyone working."

I nod, and Steven takes a deep breath and rubs his hands together. "Well - let's go. Ten minutes till we open."

Just like that, I'm thrown into a full, busy day of work, and I'm thankfully never able to stop and think much about my birthday, and the way I'm spending it.

* * * * * * * * * *

A few minutes before 10:30 PM, the restaurant is empty, with no future customers in sight. Steven clears his throat; automatically, the rest of us turn to look at him.

"Well, everything's cleaned up around here, so I think it's safe to say we can close up a couple minutes early," he says. His face is tired, but there's a look of satisfaction on it. "Thanks for the good work today, ya'll."

Everyone nods and begins exiting the kitchen - but no one seems to want to leave. They're all hanging around and talking to one another, exchanging stories about certain customers and other things that happened during the day.

Walking over to the booth where Josh has been sitting all day, I notice that he's fallen asleep on top of the table, his head resting on his arms. Shaking him gently, I whisper, "Jo - *Tom*. Time to go home. Let's go."

Josh wakes up quickly, and I help him stand up as he rubs his eyes. Leading him to the front door, we're just about to exit when I hear Steven call, "Hey, Mike! Not so fast."

I whirl around to see Steven walking towards me, a mischievous grin on his face. Frowning, I ask, "What's up?"

The rest of the group floats over as Steven simply grins at me. I tilt my head in confusion. "Come on, what's goin' on?"

"Well," says Steven, "a little bird told me your birthday's today."

I look down at Josh to see if he's involved, but his face is perfectly innocent. Looking back up at Steven, I cross my arms and nod slowly. "Yeah. It is."

"You didn't think you'd sneak off without a party, did you?" asks Davey, wrapping his arm around Ashley.

I frown. "I don't get it. What party?"

Tracy steps forward, a kind smile on her face. "Whenever anyone around here has a birthday, we take them out to celebrate."

"So, it's a good thing I knew today was your birthday, or you wouldn't have gotten a party," laughs Steven.

I let a smile creep onto my face. I'm almost too surprised to say anything, so all I can muster is, "Where are we going?"

* * * * * * * * * *

Walking into the bowling alley, the first sound to reach my ears is that of bowling pins being knocked down, the crash echoing all throughout the building. Neon lights flash brightly, and I take a moment to adjust to the lighting.

"Well," yells Steven over the noise, "here we are."

I grin and nod. Steven must notice the pained look behind my smile because he asks, "Too loud?"

"Nah," I say quickly. "It's great."

And it is - because, as if having a group of friends take me out for my birthday wasn't enough, I also have the pleasure of watching Josh take in the bowling alley, his green eyes wide in excitement. I doubt that he's ever been to a bowling alley in his life.

166

Steven leads the six of us over to the counter to pick up some bowling shoes. Then, he begins walking, not stopping until we're standing at lane number seven.

To my surprise, there's someone else standing there, too. There's a girl with long, permed black hair and sparkling brown eyes who looks to be in her mid-twenties – just about Steven's age. I'm sure she must be confused about which lane she's in - until Steven rushes up and wraps her in his arms, giving her a kiss.

I'm surprised by this, but the look on Josh's face tells me that he's twice as shocked. Keeping myself from laughing, I just pat him on the shoulder.

When the couple finishes embracing, Steven puts one arm around the girl's shoulders and looks at me, a mix of happiness and a bit of embarrassment on his face. "Mike and Tom, I want you to meet my girlfriend, Erica."

"Hey, boys," says Erica, tossing her hair and leaning into Steven as she flashes a smile.

"Hi," I manage to say.

Glancing down at Josh, I realize that he's still dumbfounded. Giving him a gentle nudge, he whispers, "Hi."

Erica laughs and rearranges her black, off-the-shoulder sweater, and Steven takes her hand. "Well - let's start playin'."

Everyone makes exclamations of agreement, and we begin our game. It's been a long time since I bowled, and I've only ever been once - but it's not me that I'm worried about. I immediately make it my prime concern to teach Josh how to bowl.

When my turn comes, I manage to keep the ball out of the gutter and end up knocking down two pins. I smile in satisfaction; even if I'm rusty at bowling, it seems my good pitching arm is still strong enough to help me. I guess Little League was good for something.

Next is Josh's turn. I wait for him to ask me for help; he does so immediately. Picking up a bright, blue-colored ball that seems a little too heavy for him, he gives me an anxious look. Standing up from where I'm sitting next to Steven, I walk over and demonstrate how to hold the ball.

"See, you put your two fingers up here, like this," I say, holding the ball up for Josh to see. "Then, you put your thumb in here. Go on."

Josh follows my lead, and then he steps forward, ready to bowl. Grabbing his right arm, I help him to release the ball. It rolls for a few seconds before ending up in the gutter.

Josh bites his lip and looks up at me, disappointment written all over his face - but I nod enthusiastically. "Yeah, yeah, that was great! Don't worry, you get to go again."

I show Josh where to find his ball, and then I help him bowl once more. This time, the ball rolls all the way, hitting one pin before falling into the gutter. Josh is so excited that he jumps up, narrowly avoiding hitting my chin with his head. "I did it! I did it, Mark!"

The second my name escapes Josh's lips, I can feel the color drain from my face. He said my name far too loudly, in front of all these people who think that my name is Mike. Turning around slowly, I steal a glance at the group.

Ashley and Tracy are busy talking, while Davey seems to interject something occasionally. I almost sigh in relief - they didn't notice anything. Then, my eyes move over to Steven and Erica.

My first glance reveals that the two of them are busy talking and looking into each other's eyes - but as I stare at Steven, I'm almost positive that he's looking at me out of the corner of his eye.

No, I think to myself. *You're just being paranoid. No one heard a thing. Besides, you're a good enough liar - you could whip up an excuse in seconds flat.*

Turning back to Josh, I realize that he's looking at me with an expression of total fear. Quickly reassuring him (and myself), I whisper, "I think we're okay. I think we're okay."

And that seems to be true - but I can't shake the feeling that Steven was watching me. Things are going so well now. I have friends, a job, a home, and even a birthday party - and I'm not willing to lose all that just because I didn't tell the truth in the first place. I lied to everyone about my name because I wanted to be careful - there's no harm in that. But now, they all know me as Mike. That's who I am now, and that's who I have to be for as long as Josh and I want to live in Andersonville. That's the game that I have to play as long as I want Josh and I to be safe and happy. It's a game I don't mind playing for long - as long as I win in the end.

CHAPTER TWENTY-SEVEN
TIM

"Good morning, church," says the pastor.

"Good morning," the church responds, almost in unison.

"Today, I'm going to talk to you about hope." The pastor looks around at everyone. "It's a hard thing to find sometimes. I'm sure all of you have been in tough situations before, where you thought that hope was an impossible thing. But the truth is that you can always find hope in Jesus."

I swallow hard and rub my hands together anxiously. I reach up to push some of my light brown hair out of my face; my hand brushes against my forehead, and I realize that I'm sweating. How long am I going to need to sit here? Thirty minutes? An hour? I'm not sure how long I can listen to the words coming out of this man's mouth - this man who seems so confident and sure of what he's saying.

"You've all heard the word 'hope' before. But have you ever thought about what it really means, and how it's used in the Bible? In the Bible, the word hope is used over 100 times. That's a lot, don't you think?"

The whole congregation nods in unison. I can't deny the truth of his words and find myself nodding as well.

"Well, it's easy to use the word 'hope' in several ways. For example, children say things like, 'I hope I get a new bike for Christmas,' and adults say things like, 'I hope this interview goes well.' But what about when nothing's going well? What about when you can't do anything about the hard situation that you're in?"

The pastor begins walking around on the platform. "The kind of hope that God gives us is a different kind of hope. It's not just the kind that you use when you're happy, or when things are easy. It's a kind that can't fade away."

Suddenly, as the pastor's words begin to settle in, I have an urge to give him my complete attention.

"The trick to finding this everlasting hope is to trust in God and to put your faith in Him. When we put our faith in earthly things, like people, we can be let down. No one is perfect, and everyone will break a promise at least once in his or her life. But when we put our faith and our trust in the Lord, He will never let us down."

I feel my breath catch in my throat. Somehow, this man is talking about the exact subject that has been on my mind for over three years - and, most recently, for the past few days. His words about promises cause my heart to begin aching as I think of the promise that I broke to Mark. The man is right - no matter what, everyone is going to let you down at some point in your life. That, I'm sure of. What I'm *not* sure of is the pastor's confidence in the fact that God won't let us down. How could he say that? Hasn't he ever had something bad happen in his life? If he had, then he would know that he's wrong.

"Life never goes perfectly. It can be easy to find our-selves blaming God for the bad things that happen in our lives - but those things aren't brought on by Him. They're brought on by the sin of the world. God doesn't *want* us to go through hard things, which is why He sent His Son to die on the cross to take the penalty for our sins. There will be a day when he defeats the devil - and death - forever, but for now, He wants to *use* the bad things that happen to us in order to bring us to Him. He uses even the bad things in life to help us. That's why we need to have hope."

My eyes begin to burn, and I rub them quickly, trying to catch my breath. I sit on the edge of my seat for the rest of the sermon, hanging onto every word, trying to process each one and apply it to my own life. Everything the pastor says seems to resonate with me. It's as if he can see into my mind and knows exactly what I'm thinking. It's like he knows all about Mark, my parents, and everything else that's happened to my family and I these past three years. I shudder as my eyes begin filling up again, and I listen closely to the pastor's every word.

Finally, after about an hour, the pastor says, "I'll leave you with this. Lamentations 3:21-24 says: This I recall to my mind, therefore I have hope. Through the Lord's mercies we are not consumed, because His compassions fail not. They are new every morning; great is Your faithfulness. 'The Lord is my portion,' says my soul, 'Therefore I hope in Him!' I hope that all of you take these words with you and remember them throughout your day. Let us pray."

The pastor finishes with a prayer, and I try hard to concentrate - but my mind is overwhelmed by all that I've heard in the past hour. As soon as the pastor finishes, the church begins to empty out - but I stay sitting for a moment. I glance around at the building, taking in its stained-glass windows and smiling people.

Part of me doesn't want to leave, because I'm afraid that when I step outside, the newfound feeling that I have will vanish. Cautiously, I stand up and begin walking, filing in behind the rest of the congregation.

Before I know it, I'm stepping outside into the cool, autumn air - and I take a deep breath, filling my lungs with it. To my surprise, the feeling doesn't go away. In fact, it becomes stronger as I begin walking down the street.

Never in my life have I heard a sermon like the one I just heard. It was nothing like I was expecting. In fact, the pastor's words were so surprising that I still haven't quite processed them all completely yet.

I had no idea that I would come out of that little church with such a new mindset. I never expected to believe the pastor at all - and yet, here I am, feeling wholeheartedly convinced that my visit to the church was not just a coincidence.

As I walk down the street, I remember my mother, and the faith she used to have. She tried her best to bring Mark and I to church as often as she could. The older we got, though, we just seemed to stop going. I'm not sure why I stopped… I don't think I had much of anything *against* going to church - it just stopped being convenient. Mark, though… Well, he was a different story. He was only ten at the time, but he began resisting our mom's invitations. It wasn't that he wanted to stay at home. In fact, he wanted to be anywhere but there… *and* church.

As much as my mom tried to convey and pass on her faith to me, I never really had any sort of faith of my own. Now, though… I think I just might.

CHAPTER TWENTY-EIGHT
TIM

It takes me over a day, but just as the sun begins to set, I spot a sign that reads: Davidson, 3 miles. Now, I know that I'm close. I'm close to Kate, the town of Davidson, and my new life. I want to confess everything to her. I didn't used to hate my lying completely, because I knew that it was necessary - but now, knowing how much I care about Kate... Well, I wouldn't feel right continuing our relationship without her knowing the truth. Things will be better when I do.

It's only been a little while since I saw the sign about Davidson, but since the sun is already setting, I know that it would be a good idea to find a place to rest for the night. Tomorrow morning, I can head straight to town - and even though I won't be with my brother, I'll be with Kate again... and that's good enough for now.

I find myself walking through a small town. Passing by shops, restaurants, and other assorted places, the town reminds me of Davidson - although it seems to be much smaller, and a bit older, but less developed. The town is definitely alive, but it seems quiet, and tired. Maybe it isn't always that way, but it sure seems like it today.

A few people pass me by, and I duck my head, trying to appear inconspicuous. All I want to do is find a place to sleep - but to do that, I'll have to walk all the way through this downtown area, and now would be a bad time to get caught.

As I walk by a restaurant, I take a moment to peer inside. It reminds me a bit of Red's Diner, back in Davidson, only a little more modern.

Glancing at my reflection in the window, I notice how tired I look - but there's something beneath that tiredness. Something... *hopeful*. I may be exhausted and worn out, but thanks to my visit to the church, I know that I can't give up on anything now.

Suddenly, I hear the restaurant door open, and a few voices flood out. "I'll see you guys tomorrow," a voice calls.

I keep my head down, trying to keep from being noticed - and that's when it happens. Looking up, I expect to see a stranger. Instead, I see a dark-haired boy with bluish-green eyes and a small smile. A boy who I know.

My heart begins pounding so loudly that I can hear it. My palms begin sweating, and I wipe them on my jeans. Squinting at the boy, it takes me a moment before I realize who I'm looking at.

Mark doesn't seem to have changed much in the past three years. Aside from getting a lot taller, his face, his posture, and everything else about him is the same. I always knew I'd recognize him in an instant if I ever saw him again. Now, although my brother and I are standing just a few feet from one another, I can't quite believe that it's him.

I wait a moment and observe the scene taking place before me. Mark is standing in front of the door to the restaurant, talking to a red-headed boy who can't be more than seven. The boy is grinning up at Mark, looking at him in admiration.

"Ready to go, Josh?" asks Mark.

I start at the sound of his voice. It's so much deeper than I last heard it - and to top it off, it's just... *different*. There's a solemn, serious sort of tone to it that was never there before. For some reason, I can't help but dislike it immediately.

"Okay," exclaims the little boy, whose voice is that of innocence and curiosity.

The pair begins walking down the sidewalk, taking absolutely no notice of me. For half a second, I watch them walk away - and then, I rush forward and exclaim, "Mark!"

Mark stops walking suddenly. Then, he turns around slowly. I watch as his eyes meet mine - and immediately, his face goes white. To my surprise, I can see a hint of fear in his eyes.

"What's wrong, Mark?" whispers the little boy. "What's going on?"

Mark waves his hand behind him, not looking at the boy. "Josh, I need you to go back inside the restaurant. Just tell everyone you're waiting for me for a second. Got it?"

Josh nods, and he walks the ten feet back to the restaurant and steps inside. Mark's eyes follow the boy as he walks. As soon as he disappears inside the building, Mark turns his attention back to me.

"Mark," I say again, stepping closer to him. "Do you remember me?" As soon as the words are out of my mouth, I realize what a dumb question this is. Of course, my own brother remembers me - how could he forget? But even as I look at Mark, I realize why I asked the question. I asked it because, although I recognize my brother, there's something different about him that I never noticed before - so, naturally, Mark must see something different about me, too.

Mark stares at me for a moment, his mouth open slightly and his eyes searching my face. Then, he says quietly, "T - Tim?"

I nod and let out the breath that I've been holding in. "Yeah," I say, cracking a smile. "It's me."

Mark swallows hard and puts a hand on his forehead, pushing his dark hair out of his face. "What..." he breathes, unable to speak.

I let out a little laugh. "It's okay. I was shocked, too." I step closer, but Mark backs away from me.

"What are you doing here?" he asks. I expect the words to come out in a simple, questioning way - but they don't. Instead, they come off as a kind of accusation.

I assume this to be thanks to Mark's shock, and I shake my head, trying to emphasize the fact that I'm feeling the same way as him. "Well, I've been looking for you. I went to Charlotte to find you, and the foster home told me you'd run away. I never expected to find you here, of all places. Oh, wow, Mark -"

I rush forward again, but like last time, Mark backs away. This time, his eyes are cold, and his face hard. "You're lying. You weren't looking for me."

The excited look on my face vanishes. "What? Of course, I was looking for you. Why would I lie about that?"

Mark shakes his head. "Why wouldn't you? You lied about everything else."

"What?" I exclaim, still confused. "What did I lie about?"

"You said you'd come for me." Mark's face is that of stone, and his eyes are cold and shifting - but there's a fire lit behind them that I know was caused by me. "You said you'd come, but you never did. I waited in all those foster homes for *three years*. I had to live a kind of hell, all by myself, because my own brother couldn't come find me. I didn't know where you were, or if you'd ever come for me. I thought about you all the time for two years - and then, I just stopped hoping... because I knew. You got a new life that you liked better, and you forgot about me. You promised, Tim. *You promised.*"

Mark's voice begins to crack strangely at these last two words, and I expect to see his eyes beginning to well with tears - but they don't. His face is void of all emotion, while his voice tells me everything I need to know.

"I'm sorry, Mark," I whisper, feeling unable to raise my voice. "I'm so sorry. I always planned to go back for you. But I was just a kid, and I had a foster family who expected me to stay with them. In fact, they wanted me to forget about my family. I didn't want to - and I swear to you, I never did. That's why I finally left. I didn't have a car or a lot of money - I just got on my bike and went to find you. And you weren't there."

To my surprise, Mark scoffs. "You were just a kid, huh? Just a kid. Just a little kid who couldn't do anything for himself." He says these words in a mocking sort of way. "Well, guess what, Tim? I'm the same age you were - and look at me." Mark spreads out his arms and motions to himself, and then to his surroundings. "I made it all the way out here by myself. I started a new life here. Maybe I'm 'just a kid,' like you say, but I did all this by myself. I've got a job, and I've got friends. I waited too long for you to just come back and be my brother again."

I begin stammering and raise my voice a bit, seeing the way the conversation is going downhill. "I - I'm sorry, Mark. I mean it. I wish I'd tried to find you earlier, and I was stupid not to. But I want you to come with me! I got a job at a grocery store in Davidson, which is just the next town over. I can take care of us. Family should be together."

Mark laughs bitterly - and suddenly, every word that comes off his tongue is like fire. "You should know that you're kidding yourself, Tim. We're not family anymore. The second you made that promise to me, I should've known you were going to break it. And because you did, we can't be family anymore. You're not my brother now - because you threw away that chance. I don't even know you. And you don't know me."

Suddenly, before I know what's happening, Mark is running. He's running fast, all the way down the street - and for some reason, I don't try to stop him.

CHAPTER TWENTY-NINE
MARK

I can't stop running. I'll never be able to stop.

I thought I was done running from my past. I thought I was okay. But what else was I supposed to do when my past ended up standing right in front of me - in the form of my brother?

When I was younger, I used to dream about what it would be like when Tim came for me. He'd arrive and give me a hug. We'd walk down the city streets, and maybe stop somewhere for ice cream. Maybe we'd even play a game of basketball. Then, we'd go home. Maybe it wouldn't be our old home - but I was okay with that. I just wanted to have a home *somewhere*.

I had always pictured Tim as the smiling, kind, good-natured fourteen-year-old who had been imprinted on my mind three years ago. For some reason, it never really occurred to me that he would look different, or even act different. It never occurred to me that *I* would be different, either. Because, when I looked at Tim, I didn't see my hero - my big brother. I only saw a person who had forgotten about me. I had expected to be happy to see him, but I hated him. Oh, I really hate him. I hate him almost as much as...

I run faster, and as I do, the sky seems to become much darker. I speed through the rest of downtown Andersonville, down a few winding streets, all the way through the woods, and finally step inside the cabin, slamming the door shut behind me.

Leaning against the door, I close my eyes and try to catch my breath. I hope Tim didn't try to follow me. I don't think he did. I've always been fast - and, besides, why would he want to catch up to me? He sure hasn't seemed to care about me for the past three years, so why would he start now?

Walking over to the couch, I sit down and rest my head in my hands. I scan the room, trying to find something to distract myself - but there's nothing to help me. All I can see is Tim's face - a face that I can't recognize.

I saw a lot of emotions in Tim's face. There was excitement, shock, and a whole lot of other things, too. There may have even been some hurt. But all I really saw was the face of the brother who abandoned me. I hate that face. I hate it.

I feel a lump form in my throat, and my breathing quickens. I wipe my eyes and take a deep breath. The only tears I'm crying are tears of anger - nothing else.

I swallow hard. Tim can go ahead and find someone else to be his brother - 'cause it's not gonna be me. I don't care about him. I just hate him. I hate him so much. "To hell with him," I whisper, breaking the cabin's eerie silence. The words feel good - but they don't help much. All I want is for Tim to disappear. I wish he didn't exist. I'd pray for some kind of miracle, but I haven't done that in years, and I don't intend to now.

Exhausted, I lie down on my back and close my eyes. My eyelids get heavier, and heavier...

There's a knock at the door, and I sit up straight. Rubbing my eyes, I realize how dark it is outside. I must've fallen asleep, though I don't know for how long.

For a moment, I wonder what I'm doing here, and I forget everything that's happened - and then, it hits me. This also causes me to realize that there's a good chance that the person at the door is Tim.

Running to the window, I peer through it - and instead of seeing Tim, I see Josh... and none other than Steven.

Shocked, I walk over to the door and open it. "Uh - I... Steven, what're you doin' here?"

Steven gives Josh a gentle push to usher him inside, and Josh obeys. "Mike, can I talk to you for a second?"

I shrug, still trying to figure out why Steven is here. "Um - sure."

There's a long pause. Then, Steven asks, "Outside?"

I nod. "Oh. Yeah." Turning to Josh, I say, "I'll be right out here."

Josh nods, and I shut the door behind me. Now, it's just me and Steven.

"So," I say, stuffing my hands in my pockets and forcing a small, casual smile, "what're you doin' here?"

"Well, first off, I came to drop off Tom," explains Steven. "You left him at the restaurant."

Suddenly, I remember, and I smack my forehead. "Oh, man… I'm sorry, Steven. I was busy, and I just forgot that he was there." I take a good look at Steven. He's always seemed trustworthy to me - but the fact that he knows where Josh and I live isn't good news. Hurriedly, I try to rush him off. "Well… thanks for bringing him by."

I turn to walk inside the house, but Steven stops me. "Mark."

At the sound of my name on Steven's lips, my heart begins thumping so loudly that I can hear it in my ears. "What'd you call me?" I gasp.

Steven crosses his arms and looks closely at me. "I heard Tom call you that at the bowling alley. Then, he called you that again at the restaurant when he asked me to take him home. I know that your real name is Mark."

I start laughing nervously, desperate to keep Steven from learning the truth. "What? You must've just heard him wrong. I mean, the name 'Mike' sounds pretty close to 'Mark.' You just heard him wrong - that's all."

Steven sighs. Then, suddenly, he says, "I've never told you much about my life. A lot happened to me before I came to Andersonville, and… I want you to hear about it."

I shrug. "You don't need to tell me anything."

"But I want to. Just… promise me you'll listen, and that you'll hear me out all the way."

I nod slowly. There can't be any harm in just listening. "Alright."

Steven takes a deep breath. I can see beads of sweat beginning to form on his forehead, and he wipes them away hastily, brushing his dark hair out of his face. "Okay. Well… I grew up in a pretty big family. Life was okay when I was a little kid - but it got worse as time went on. My dad had fought in Vietnam all the way to about halfway through the war, and he couldn't seem to get it out of his head. He had PTSD (that's an acronym for 'post-traumatic stress disorder') and was always having flashbacks."

Steven pauses for a moment to look at me, and I avoid his gaze. After another second, he continues. "My mom was always trying to help him, but he didn't want her help. He started drinking, saying that it was the best form of medicine he could possibly have. When I was about twelve, it got to the point where he couldn't stop. Then, he started having problems. He was always angry. He'd always had a bad temper, but he couldn't keep it under control anymore. He started taking things out on me. So, when I was fifteen, I left home."

My breathing quickens suddenly, and I listen closely as Steven continues. "I'd been gone for a long time when one day, I saw an article in the paper. It was about a car crash caused by a drunk driver that had taken place just the day before. And I hated myself, because I thought that if I had just been there, I could have stopped it. I could have stopped it all."

I can feel my chest begin heaving. I force myself to look up at Steven's face - and I find myself looking at a ghost.

Without a word, I open the door and rush inside the cabin, slamming the door shut behind me.

I run straight to my room, and as soon as I enter it, I drag my backpack out from under my bed. Then, I begin angrily stuffing my clothes and other belongings inside it, barely able to focus on what I'm doing, just moving mechanically.

Just as I finish packing, Josh steps into the room. Stealing a quick glance at his freckled face, I'm sure that he didn't hear the conversation - but he still looks concerned.

"Mark? What's going on?" he asks in a timid voice.

I avoid his gaze and sling my backpack over my shoulders. "Josh, go pack your stuff. We're leaving."

Glancing at Josh out of the corner of my eye, I notice the mix of shock and confusion that has appeared on his face. His mouth is hanging open slightly, and his big, green eyes are wider than usual.

"Well, go on," I say impatiently. "Go pack."

Josh shakes his head slowly; he's rooted to the spot. "I…" he whispers. "I don't want to."

I shrug, unfazed by Josh's reluctance. "Time to go, then. Get something to eat, and we'll leave."

I move to leave my room, but suddenly, Josh steps in front of the door, blocking me. "What's going on, Mark? Why do we have to leave?"

I take Josh by the shoulder and try to move him gently out of the way. "You've gotta let me through, Josh."

"No!" exclaims Josh. He says this so firmly that I step back in surprise. Then, he says, "I'm not going to let you through until you tell me what's going on."

I take a moment to look closely at the little boy. He looks so determined that I'm not sure I'd be able to go much longer without giving him some sort of explanation - so, I take a deep breath and turn away from him. Walking over to the bedroom window, I peer out of it, worried that Steven might be hanging around and trying to listen to us talk. There's no sign of him, but I close the curtains anyway.

Sitting down on my bed, I lean forward and make eye contact with Josh. Then, in a voice barely above a whisper, I say, "You know that guy who I was talking to earlier, outside the restaurant?"

Josh nods. Then, I say, "Well - he's my brother."

I watch as Josh's eyes bug out in surprise. He stares at me for a moment, obviously shocked. Then, he asks, "Your brother? Well - what was he doing there?"

"He said he came to look for me. You see, Josh…" I take a deep breath. I have to tell him the truth. I have to if I'm going to make him understand. "When my parents died three years ago, my brother and I were separated. He said he'd come back for me, but he never did. So, I hadn't seen him in three years… until now."

Josh shakes his head in confusion. "Why aren't you happy about that? Didn't you miss him?"

I look away. "Yeah, I missed him. For a long time. But I stopped when I realized that he wasn't coming back for me. You may not understand right now, but I just have to get out of here. I don't want to see him ever again. I don't want him to come looking for me. So, we need to leave - and we can't come back."

"But I'm sure he doesn't know we're living here," exclaims Josh. "Why can't we stay?"

I glance in the direction of the front door and shudder. Shaking my head, I stand up. "We just can't. It's not safe here anymore."

Josh lets his head fall, and I realize that this might be too much for Josh to understand or handle. Patting him on the shoulder, I say, "I'm sorry, Josh. I'm sorry for leaving you at the restaurant earlier, and I'm sorry that all this is happening. But we have to go right now."

Rushing past Josh and into the kitchen, I grab some food and stuff it into my backpack. Then, I peer out through the front window, just to make sure that Steven is gone for good. Again, he's nowhere to be seen - so, as soon as Josh shows up beside me, I open the front door and begin running.

CHAPTER THIRTY
TIM

I walk slowly into the town of Davidson, my head bent, and my hands stuffed in my pockets. Just yesterday, I was ecstatic to be headed back to Davidson; now, it couldn't matter less to me.

Staring up at the cold, cloudy autumn sky, I try to wrap my head around the events of the past few hours. Finding Mark was the best thing that could've happened to me - but it turned out to be the very opposite.

Passing by Davidson Bible Church, I give the building a hard look and feel a lump rise in my throat. What was the use of finding hope in God when He decided to let everything fall apart? Why would He let me find my brother just for him to reject me?

I can't get Mark's face out of my head. He was so... so *different*. His eyes were cold, his face hard, and he looked to be older than fourteen. Everything about him was a sure sign to me that he's been hurting for a long time. What's worse is that I could've stopped all that pain if I'd only decided to find him earlier. Now, he's the one hurting me - and I guess it's only fair.

A drop of rain hits my forehead, and I look up angrily at the sky. *Why couldn't things work out for me? Just once, why couldn't life be easy?*

Just as these thoughts are running through my head, I look to the right and realize that I'm standing outside of Red's Diner. Swallowing hard, I walk over to the window and peer inside.

The warm glow of yellow lights is flooding the building, which is filled with smiling faces. Among these faces, I don't see a single familiar one - until my eyes land on the face of the only person in the world I care about besides Mark: my girlfriend.

Kate is sitting in a booth, talking to her cousin Susan - or rather, I should say *listening*, since Susan appears to be doing all the talking. This surprises me; after all, isn't Kate the chatterbox? Isn't she the one who's always filled with life and excitement? Apparently, she isn't today, because the look on her face is one of a person trying hard not to look sad. I've felt that look before on myself, and I hate seeing it on Kate.

I stand outside the restaurant for a couple minutes, simply observing Kate and trying to decide whether I should go inside. Suddenly, the rain begins to pour down hard, making my decision for me. I'm just about to walk over to the door when, for some reason, Kate's head turns, and her eyes meet mine. As soon as she sees me, her face lights up. In spite of my feelings about Mark, I smile back.

I move to go inside, but before I know what's happening, she's getting up from her booth and running to the door.

The next thing I know, she's outside, standing in front of me in the pouring rain, and all I want to do is tell her how much I love her. Instead, I simply let her rush forward, and she wraps her arms around me.

When she steps back, she begins talking quickly - and I'm reassured that she's still the same Kate Woodland I remember.

"What are you doing here?" she asks. "When I didn't hear from you, I assumed you'd left to visit colleges, so I didn't worry - but I had no idea when you'd be back. So - where have you been?"

I take a moment to look at her flushed, happy face. Her hair is almost totally soaked now and hanging over her shoulders, but she doesn't seem to mind. Her green eyes are locked with mine, and I wish I could look into those eyes forever. I wish I didn't have to ruin this moment by telling Kate the truth.

"Listen, Kate," I say slowly, "I haven't been honest with you."

Kate is still smiling. She shakes her head. "What do you mean?"

"I mean…" I hesitate and run my hands through my wet hair, trying to think of what to say. "I didn't tell you the truth about my life."

Now, Kate's smile begins melting slowly. "What? What did you lie about?"

I stare at Kate for one moment more. I have to tell her everything. It's now or never. Before I lose my nerve, I begin talking quickly. "I don't live with my parents. They died three years ago. I'm on my own. I ran away from my foster family's home because I wanted to find my brother. We were separated when our parents died, and I promised him I would go back for him. So that's where I've been - in Charlotte."

Kate's face is blank. Worried, I begin talking even faster. "Kate, I wanted to tell you the truth this whole time, but I was afraid the police would find me and bring me back to my foster parents, and I couldn't live with myself if I let that happen, because my brother is all alone out there, and it's my job to find him. I'm so sorry that I wasn't honest with you, but now that you know the truth, can't you understand?"

I wait anxiously for Kate to nod, or smile, or give me a few words of encouragement. Instead, I feel my heart sink as she shakes her head and takes a step backwards.

"What's your name?" she asks slowly.

"Tim Ryder."

"Are you sure?"

"Yes. My name is Timothy Andrew Ryder, and I never lied about that," I say, trying to remain calm but noticing the way Kate is backing towards the restaurant door. "I told you my real name because I was sure I could trust you. In fact, everyone who I've met in Davidson knows my real name, and they all could've looked me up at any time. I'm sure the police are still looking for me. Anyone could turn me in at any time, even though I haven't done anything wrong. So, you see? I told you my name because I was never worried. I trusted you - and now, I realize that you have the same right to be able to trust me and know the truth about myself."

"I need proof," says Kate, her voice wavering.

"Okay, okay," I say quickly, digging into my pocket. Immediately, I retrieve my driver's license and hold it out for Kate to see. "There's my name, right there, see? Timothy Andrew Ryder, born July 20th, 1969. See? It's all legal, and you could take it to the nearest police station and ask them to prove that. I don't mind... I just want you to believe me."

"But what about your story?" asks Kate. She could open the restaurant door at any moment now, but she hasn't moved for a few seconds. "How am I supposed to know that's real?"

"Go find out about me at a police station," I say, hating the words as I say them but knowing that they're necessary to gain Kate's trust. "Just ask them if they've heard of me. You'll find information in seconds flat, I swear."

"How could you swear to anything?" asks Kate, her voice raising slowly. "How could you promise anything? We've known each other for months, and you've lied that whole time. I don't really know who you are."

"Yes, yes you do," I say quickly, beginning to feel panicked. "You know all about me - maybe not about my past, but about who I am as a person. And that's another reason why I lied. I wanted you to get to know *me*, and not my past, Kate."

"But - but you lied about *everything*. You met my family, but I never met yours. I just assumed that they were busy, like you said."

Kate's voice is strained now, to the point where I think she might be crying - although I can't tell, since we're standing in the rain. Instinctively, I take a step forward to comfort her, but she backs further away. The movement sends a dagger through my heart as I realize that Mark reacted to me that way, too. Everyone I love in the world is now backing away from me instead of running towards me - and the thought scares me.

"Kate, I'm so sorry," I say, but Kate shakes her head.

"Don't talk to me anymore, Tim," she exclaims. Before I can say another word, she rushes inside the restaurant, leaving me by myself in the pouring rain.

CHAPTER THIRTY-ONE
TIM

It hurts enough to be rejected by one person - but to be rejected by two, and in one day? I'm not sure I've ever felt so low in my life.

Mark and Kate were the two people left in my life who I truly cared about. All others either died or forfeited the right to be considered as people I love. But Mark and Kate were different. Mark was my little brother - the little kid who I was forced to leave three years ago. I was expecting to find him as that same kid, eager and overjoyed to see me - but I couldn't have been more wrong.

I never expected to meet a girl like Kate. She was so full of joy and had a love for life. When I arrived in Davidson and laid my eyes on her again, I was sure that things would be fine. Now, she's rejected me, too - and I have no one left.

This is all I can think about as I try to fall asleep on a bench under a gazebo in the park. Since I'm out of money and out of a job, I'm not sure what to do or where to go next.

Shivering and exhausted from the day's events, I quickly drift off to sleep, and I don't wake up until late the next morning.

Although I know I need to leave town, my feet begin leading me blindly. I'm unsure of where I'm going until I find myself standing in front of Kate's house.

I can't go inside. I can't force myself to talk to Kate again. Even though I wish I could make her understand, I know that it's not fair for me to push any harder. I need to leave and forget about Kate - and I need to let her forget about me, too.

I'm just about to begin walking down the street when Kate's front door swings open. The next thing I know, I'm looking into Kate's big, green eyes. They look a bit red and raw, as if she didn't get much sleep last night.

Kate stuffs her hands in her jean jacket pockets and looks closely at me. "Hi."

I swallow hard. "Hi."

Kate takes in my backpack and tired expression for a moment. Then, she asks, "Where are you going?"

I shrug, trying to appear nonchalant. "I don't know. Anywhere."

Kate stares at her feet for a moment. Then, she says quickly, "Tim, I'm willing to hear your story again. But this time, I need to hear *all* of it - every detail."

Unable to conceal my sudden excitement, I nod eagerly. "Yeah, yeah, I promise. I'll tell you everything if you really want to listen."

Kate nods and purses her lips, her face void of emotion. Then, the two of us walk up to her front porch and sit down on a couple of white wicker chairs.

"So," I say, taking a deep breath, "where do you want me to start?"

"From the beginning," says Kate.

I allow a little laugh to escape from my lips. "So, the day I was born?"

Kate simply stares at me, not even cracking a smile. Awkwardly, I clear my throat and nod. "Alright. Um... I guess it started three years ago. My family lived in Charlotte. It was just my parents, my brother and I. My parents died in a car crash that year. I was fourteen, and my brother was ten. It all happened so fast, and before I knew it, I was sent off to live with a foster family, while my brother was forced to stay back in the city."

I glance at Kate to see if she's listening. She nods, and I continue. "I promised my brother that I would go back for him one day. I really did mean it, but I was just a kid - and things didn't work out the way I planned. My new foster parents didn't encourage me to keep in touch with my brother. I wanted to, but even when I tried, my letters must have never made it to him, because I never got any in return. Anyways, in September, I ran away to find my brother - but on the way, one of my bike tires got punctured. I stopped in Davidson to earn money for a new one, but I ended up going by bus instead. So, I went to the foster home where my brother used to live, and they told me he ran away a few months ago."

I take another glance at Kate. Her blank expression has begun to transform into one of concern, which encourages me to continue. "I'd just about given up when, on my way back here, I passed my brother on the sidewalk. I couldn't believe my eyes. He was taller, but I knew it was him. I was so excited, I started talking to him... but he turned me away. He was angry that I'd left him alone for so long. I tried to explain, but he ran away from me. So, I came back here. And that... that just about covers everything."

I take a long, deep breath. Kate's face is now full of a mix of concern, pity, and understanding. Still, though, she doesn't say anything.

"So," I say, chancing to ask the question that I've been wanting to ask all this time, "do you believe me?"

Slowly, Kate begins nodding. "Yeah. I think I do."

"And..." I hesitate. "Do you think you could forgive me?"

Again, Kate nods. I can feel a grin begin spreading across my face, and I send up a silent *thank you*.

"So," says Kate, leaning forward and letting her reddish-blonde hair fall over her shoulders, "if you're willing to let a few other people get to know you, my family's having Thanksgiving dinner tomorrow. If you want to come..."

"Yes," I answer immediately, eager to accept her forgiveness (and her invitation). "Thanks, Kate."

* * * * * * * * * *

"Tim, are you coming?"

I look up from the book I'm holding to make eye contact with Kate across the room. She's wearing a pretty sweater the color of red autumn leaves, and a white skirt to go with it.

"'Course," I reply, standing up and making my way over to her. "You know," I chance suddenly, taking her by the hand, "you look so beautiful."

Kate's cheeks go bright pink, but she smiles and doesn't say anything. Although I've told Kate the truth, and she made it clear that she's forgiven me, she still seems to be acting so careful around me.

Yesterday, after Kate and I talked, we went inside her house, where I "reintroduced" myself to her family. To my surprise, her parents were kind and welcoming though not without a bit of hesitation, and as soon as I finished the second round of telling my story, they promised not to turn me in or tell anyone about my past. They said that it was up to me to tell others my story. Then, they offered me their guest room which was Andy's room before he moved to the dorm.

Kate and I then spent the rest of the day getting to know each other better. I told her all about myself, and my brother - but I left out most of what my life was like before the accident. That, she didn't need to know.

Now, most of Kate's family is here to celebrate Thanksgiving. Her family from Kentucky arrived last night and stayed in a hotel, while the rest already live in Davidson. The second they all walked through the door, I almost felt too overwhelmed to say anything - so I simply greeted each one of them and tried to keep to myself. Now that we're about to eat, though, I'm not sure I'll be able to avoid talking to them.

We walk over to the dining room, where a turkey surrounded by dressing is already sitting on the table - and where the table is crowded with various relatives, including Kate's parents, aunts, uncles, and cousins. On one side of the table sits Susan, her parents, and her nineteen-year-old brother Drew. On the other side sits Kate's two basketball-loving teenage cousins Clark and Ned from Kentucky, along with their parents. Mr. and Mrs. Woodland are sitting next to each other on the far end of the table, so Kate and I sit down on the other.

Every grown-up pair of eyes at the table seems to be fixed on me, so I swallow hard and give everyone a little nod and a forced smile. I met everyone when they arrived about a half an hour ago, but it's still a lot of people who I barely know. Kate gives me a knowing smile; I know she can tell exactly how I'm feeling right now.

After Mr. Woodland says the blessing and we begin eating, everyone seems to be involved in a conversation except for me. Kate is sitting to my left, and the people nearest to her are her cousins Clark and Ned, so she's busy talking to them. They're mostly talking about basketball. Even though I like basketball and could easily join their conversation, I don't feel like it. I've never been a very shy person or anything like that - but suddenly, I feel almost intimidated by all of Kate's family here in one place. Who knows what Kate's said to them about me - or what Kate's parents have said.

"So, Tim."

I look up from my plate of food to see Kate's uncle - Susan's dad - staring at me.

Swallowing the mashed potatoes in my mouth, I put a smile on my face. "Yes, sir?"

"Call me Thomas. We've heard a lot about you from Kate. It sounds like you're a hardworking guy."

I smile, not quite sure of what to say. So, I simply reply, "Yeah, I'm grateful to have my job."

"How's school going for you these days?"

With a sigh, I shrug. "Pretty good. Feeling ready to graduate."

"You won't have to wait much longer, will you? Almost finished. I remember my senior year; everyone was just ready to be done."

I blush. Suddenly, I realize something. It's true that I'm a senior - but I'm also a dropout. I was so close to graduating that it pains me to think about it.

"Yeah," I reply, swallowing hard.

Thomas nods and turns to his food for a moment, and I breathe a little sigh of relief. It's exhausting, trying to avoid telling everything about myself while still being honest. It's hard to resist the urge to stretch the truth now that I've been doing it so easily for so long - but I have to be honest from here on out.

As Thomas begins talking to Mr. Woodland, I turn back to my own plate of food and find myself listening to the conversation Kate is having with her sixteen-year-old cousin,

Ned, whose dark green button-down shirt is the exact color of Kate's eyes.

"They were just touring this year," Ned is saying in a southern accent much thicker than mine or Kate's. "Didn't you hear? Thought you might've."

Kate shakes her head, a surprised look on her face. "What month did they come by?"

"Well, they were in Kentucky in July. I took Tiffany to see them."

"Tiffany? Your girlfriend?"

A small smile appears on Ned's face, and he looks away and nods. "Yeah. Anyways, I thought they might have stopped in North Carolina. Maybe Tim heard about them."

I look up suddenly at the sound of my name, pretending not to have been listening to the conversation. "What's that?"

"Oh, Ned was just saying that Journey's been touring all over the country this year," says Kate, sighing. "I don't know how I could've missed them!"

I frown. "No, I didn't hear about that. I love their music, though."

Ned's brown eyes light up. "Aw, yeah? You're into music?"

"Totally. Do you like Huey Lewis and the News?"

"Yeah! Oh, man, have you heard their latest album? It's seriously good."

As Ned and I continue our conversation, with Kate and Clark joining in occasionally, I can't help but marvel at the way Kate's big family laughs and talks. They all seem so comfortable and happy around one another. It's been a long time since I truly celebrated Thanksgiving - and even though I'm grateful to be with Kate's family for the day, I can't help but wonder what Mark is doing right now.

CHAPTER THIRTY-TWO
MARK

Josh and I have been walking for two days.

I know that we're getting closer to South Carolina every day - but we still have a long way to go. Still, I know that I can't rush Josh. He may be advanced for his age, but he's still just a little kid.

Besides, I don't see too much of a need to rush, especially since Steven and Tim don't know where we're going. As far as the two of them know, Josh and I are still in Andersonville. If either of them tries looking for us at the cabin, though, they'll be out of luck - and they'll have no idea where we are.

I sigh and glance down at Josh as we walk down the street through some dark, nameless town. I can't help feeling angry with myself at the fact that this is the exact reason why I ran away from Bentwood Foster Home in the first place. I wanted a fresh start, with no reminders of my past. I wanted to be a different person. I was so close to succeeding at this goal once I adopted a new name. But things just didn't work out.

Josh and I walk a few more minutes before we enter a rural neighborhood. The grass is covered in dried leaves, and the second Josh and I step onto it, I wince at the crunching sound they make.

Noticing a farmhouse in the distance, I try to be extra quiet, keenly aware that someone inside the house could wake up at any moment. Passing the house, we walk about ten minutes more, still concealed by darkness, when suddenly, the silence around us is shattered by the wailing of sirens.

A little while later, we approach the highway, and I notice flashing red and blue lights. Just about ten feet in front of us is a road filled with people - and at the center, two mangled cars.

For a moment, I stand where I am, too dumbstruck to move. Then, I take off running, desperate to get as far away from the accident as I can.

Before I know it, I've run far enough away that I can't see the lights anymore. Leaning against a tree for support, I close my eyes and try to breathe. *Breathe in for five seconds, breathe out for five seconds.* It doesn't help. It never helps.

An image flashes through my mind, and my eyes fly wide open as I try to forget about it. I have to forget about it… but I can't. I'll never be able to.

A pain sears through my head, and I squeeze my eyes shut in agony. It's never been this bad. They said it would stop after a year or so - but it's been three.

I slide down against the tree and sit on the grass, my heart racing, and a lump rising in my throat. It used to be just mild headaches. Now it's flashbacks too, and it's hard for me to sleep - and the headaches are getting worse and worse.

I remember the way the doctors tried to explain it to my ten-year-old self. "It may be severe... migraines... nightmares... panic attacks... intense anger."

They said it might help to talk about it. They said that I needed to 'confront my emotions.' But I was just a ten-year-old kid - how was I supposed to do that? I was still processing the fact that I'd just been in a car crash - and I wasn't even able to fathom the fact that my parents were gone.

I never told anyone back in Charlotte that I have extreme Post-Traumatic Stress Disorder. Now, I wonder if talking about it would have helped me move on. I wonder if it would've taken away the pain.

My headache begins to ease, and I take a deep breath and scoff. Maybe talking about it *would've* taken away the pain... but it sure wouldn't have erased the memories.

Suddenly, as I'm beginning to calm down, Josh rushes up to me. That's when I realize that I left him behind when I ran off.

"Mark?" he says, standing a few feet away from me, a concerned look on his face. "Are you okay?"

I put a hand to my forehead and try to stand up. Struggling to my feet, I say, "Yeah. I'm fine."

The look on Josh's face tells me that he doesn't believe me. He doesn't know that I have PTSD and panic attacks - and I'm not going to tell him now. "Seriously, Josh," I say, putting on a smile and giving his shoulder a pat. "You've gotta trust me. Let's keep moving, okay?"

Josh nods and follows behind me.

* * * * * * * * *

We walk till the sun begins to come up. Then, we find a place to sleep in the woods. Although Josh drifts off to sleep right away, I don't. I'm exhausted, and I'd desperately like to sleep - but I can't. If my panic attacks are back, then that means my nightmares might be, too. The last thing I want is to wake up in a cold sweat and have Josh wonder what's wrong with me.

I sit and watch the sun come up, its light filtering through the almost-bare branches above me. My eyes burn from exhaustion, but I don't close them for a second. It's safer to stay awake. Besides, that way, I can make sure that Josh is okay.

It's too late for me to tell him what's going on. Even if I knew he'd understand, I think I'd still be too afraid to admit what I'm going through. I just want to forget about it - and getting as far away from Steven and Tim as I can will help me do just that.

* * * * * * * * *

Two days later, Josh and I have traveled even further, and although I know that we won't be able to stop until we cross into South Carolina, I'm feeling safer by the second. Despite this, though, I can't get the events of two days ago out of my head.

Walking through a busy town, I keep my head down, but can't help observing the sights around me. Coming out of the downtown area, Josh and I pass a small, brick elementary school. That's when a memory hits me.

It was mine and Tim's first day of school. I was starting first grade, and I was terrified. I was a quiet kid, though, so I hadn't said a word about it all summer.

I'd been in the classroom barely half an hour when something set me off. I don't quite remember what it was, but it made me angry. I lost my temper and went running out of my classroom, so upset that I wasn't sure where I was going. As I was running, I ended up colliding into Tim, who had just stood up from leaning over the water fountain.

"Whoa, there," he said. Then, he looked closely and realized who I was. "Mark? Why're you running?"

I crossed my arms, my face red. "I got mad."

Tim shrugged. "So? How come you're not in your classroom?"

"'Cause I didn't wanna be in there anymore." I said this as if it were the simplest thing in the world - as if a six-year-old kid could decide when he could leave the classroom.

Tim shook his head. "Cut it out, Mark. You don't just run away when you get mad."

I made a face at my big brother. "Why not?"

Tim rolled his eyes. "I get mad sometimes, but I don't run away from my problems. You've gotta face up to them."

I shrugged, unconvinced. Suddenly, a grin appeared on Tim's face, and he said, "Besides - if you don't face up to your problems, you're gonna be labeled as a little baby for the rest of your life. You don't want that, do you?"

Tim had just used the perfect tactic to convince me to behave. As a nervous six-year-old, the last thing I wanted was to be called a baby. Giving in, I nodded slowly. "Okay."

Tim walked me back to my classroom, and I spent the rest of the day trying to prove that I wasn't a baby. I wasn't a coward, and I could face up to my own problems. Like Tim had told me, I couldn't run away from my problems anymore.

My brother had helped my six-year-old self start school. He always looked out for me. He always did what was best for me.

I swallow hard and glance back at the school. Maybe Tim abandoned me - but he gave me some good advice. He told me not to run away from my problems. For a long time, I listened to his words - but not anymore. Haven't I been running away from my problems all this time? I've been so afraid of facing my past that my first instinct was to run away. I ran from Tim, and I ran from Steven. I'm not brave anymore.

I glance down at the red-haired kid walking next to me. He's only seven years old. He doesn't deserve to be dragged around with me, just because I can't face up to my past.

I've been so worried about doing what *I* want that I haven't been doing what's best for Josh. I know that now. I never asked Josh whether he *wanted* to go. In fact, I made him.

I stop walking suddenly. I can't move another step until I ask Josh what *he* wants. Even if he wants to go back, I'll have to be okay with it - because it's the right thing to do.

Josh is still walking when he realizes that I've fallen behind. Turning around, he stares at me, confused. "Mark? What is it?"

I open my mouth, but no words come out. My palms begin sweating, and I wipe them on my jeans. I take a deep breath. I have to ask him. It can't be all about me anymore. I have to be fair to Josh. I have to be a good 'brother.'

"Josh," I say slowly, "do you want to go back?"

Josh's green eyes widen, and he walks towards me. "What do you mean? I thought you said you couldn't stay back there. You said it wasn't safe, because of your -"

"I know what I said," I interrupt. "But I never asked what *you* wanted. Be honest with me, Josh. Do you want to go back or not?"

Josh studies my face for a moment, as if trying to decide if I really mean what I'm saying. Then, he answers, "Yeah. I... I liked it there."

I bite my lip. I should have known he'd say that. Still, I told myself I'd be fair to him - so I have to take him back. "Okay," I say, taking him by the shoulder. "Let's go."

CHAPTER THIRTY-THREE
MARK

It's a Tuesday morning, and the sun has been up for a few hours when we approach the familiar patch of woods surrounding the cabin. Although every step I take means that I'm getting closer to Steven (and, in that way, my past), I simply look down at Josh, take in his happy face, and am reminded that I'm doing this all for him. Seeing how happy he's been since I told him we could go back, I know for sure now that I'm doing the right thing.

The last thing I want to do is make Josh unhappy - even if it means I have to face up to my own fears. Josh is the kid here, and I'm supposed to be there for him, and make the right choices for him - not the other way around.

My only concern is the matter of making money. Now that I know I can't work for Steven anymore, I'll have to find some other job. I have experience working in a restaurant, so maybe that will help me get an interview someplace else… but I don't know. Anyways, that will have to wait for a little while. Josh and I will need to lay low for about a week, just to make sure that Steven doesn't know we've come back.

I decide to voice this to Josh, just so he knows what to expect. "Josh?"

He looks up. "Yeah?"

I bite my lip, trying to figure out how to put my thoughts into words. "Listen… We're gonna have to stay hidden for a little while, alright?"

Josh frowns. "How come?"

I hesitate. "Well… because of my brother."

Josh shakes his head. "Oh, that's no problem. He won't be able to find us here."

I turn my face away and don't say anything for a moment, unable to explain. Then, I turn back to Josh. "Just… promise me you won't go looking for anyone that we know. Okay? I'm going to get a new job, and a new name. You'll have to stay at the house, just to be safe, but I won't work long hours anymore. I'll come home early, and we'll do stuff together."

I can hear a little sigh escape from Josh's lips, and he raises his eyebrows. "Like what?"

I begin racking my mind for something to say. "Uh… We could go to the movies! Yeah, I made enough money for that at my old job. We'll go to the movies sometimes and do lots of fun stuff - you'll see."

I wait anxiously for Josh's reply. I can almost see the wheels in his brain turning, as if he's not quite sure he's satisfied with my answer. Finally, he nods and gives me a smile. "Okay."

Patting his back, I say, "Thanks, Josh."

We walk a few minutes more, and right around this time, I realize that we must be nearing the cabin. It'll come into view any second now. One... two...

I stop walking suddenly and practically dive behind the nearest tree. "Josh," I hiss, seeing that the little boy is still standing in plain sight. "Get over here."

Josh gives me a confused look - and then, I see him take in what my eyes just saw a moment ago. He obeys and runs to stand next to me.

Peering out from around the tree, I can see the cabin - and parked in front of it, a police car and a brown sedan.

My heart is beating so loudly that I can hear it in my ears. My forehead is sweating, and I wipe it with the back of my hand. "Come on," I whisper to Josh. I begin to run, and Josh follows.

We don't stop running until we've reached the edge of the woods, back where we came from a few minutes ago. Then, panting, I lean against the nearest tree and slap my forehead with my hand.

"I should've known this would happen," I groan. "Someone found out about us."

Josh, whose eyes are wide with fear at this point, whispers, "Do - do you think it was Steven?"

I swallow hard and shake my head. As much as I've been afraid of talking to Steven, my biggest fear has never been that he would turn Josh and I in. Still - I can't be sure of anything right now. "I don't know."

"What're we gonna do?" whimpers Josh.

I take in the little boy's pale face and nervous expression for a moment. I've never seen him this scared before. We need to get help - and fast. Because I have no idea what to do.

Suddenly, it hits me. Even though it'll be a risk, it's one I have to take. It could keep Josh and I safe - and maybe even help us find someplace else to go.

"Come on," I say. "We need to find Steven."

CHAPTER THIRTY-FOUR
TIM

It's been a week since I arrived back in Davidson, and those seven days have flown by. The first was spent eating Thanksgiving dinner with the Woodlands, and the second stopping by the store to ask Mr. Kilmer for my job back.

Luckily, he welcomed me back eagerly and let me start right away, allowing me to earn enough money to rent a room at the YMCA again. With work in the afternoons on weekdays, and then most of the day during the weekend, I still had plenty of free time - so, for that first week, I spent my days at the library. Part of me wished I could enroll at Kate's school - but another part of me knew the truth. If I was going to live on my own, I would have to stay under the radar till my eighteenth birthday.

So, I spent my time reading as much as I could, trying to recover a bit of the knowledge that I'd forgotten (or hadn't learned) in the past few months. Then, I went to work. When that was done, I spent every night with Kate, either eating a meal with her family or taking a walk. The more time that went by, the more that she seemed to truly forgive me. She seemed more comfortable with me, and I loved her more than ever. Although I wanted to say this to her more than once, I never had the nerve. I just tried to show her how much I cared about her.

Tonight, Kate asked me if I'd like to meet some of her friends. I said that sounded cool, and now, we're walking to a 1950s-style soda shop. As we enter the shop, we're waved over to a large table, where six people are already sitting.

Two are the couple who I met that day at the roller rink. It takes me a moment to remember their names. Kate, seeing that I'm struggling at this, reintroduces them to me as Jennifer and Scott.

The other person I already know is Kate's cousin, Susan. Having met her twice already (the second time being at Thanksgiving), we greet each other with smiles and looks of recognition.

The three other people are unfamiliar to me, and Kate introduces them to me in more detail.

"Tim," she says, motioning towards a tall guy with blond, shaggy hair, "this is Charles McKay. He's in my grade at Roosevelt."

Charles shakes my hand firmly. His letterman jacket and build both hint at the fact that he might be a football player. I'm just about to ask this very thing when Susan interjects excitedly, "He's a football player."

"Oh, yeah?" I say. "What position?"

"Quarterback," replies Charles, straightening up a bit. I notice the way his eyes dart towards Susan, who's staring at him as if he's some sort of Greek god.

The next person I meet is Mallory Namath. She has coffee-colored skin, shoulder-length dark hair, and hazel eyes, and is introduced to me as a junior who happens to be Susan's best friend.

The last person I meet is Jack Wiley, a junior with reddish hair and blue eyes. He says hardly a word to me, making me wonder if he's unfriendly or simply shy. As the evening goes on, I decide on the second option.

After about an hour of talking, I hear Scott say from down at the other end of the table, "There's a live band coming and everything. I heard they played at Jefferson once, and they were awesome."

"Oh, you're going to have to help me with my makeup, Jennifer," exclaims Susan, leaning forward. "You do yours so well."

Confused, I lean over to my right and whisper to Kate, "What're they talkin' about?"

"Oh, just the winter formal. It's next weekend," she replies.

Five minutes later, when everyone says goodbye and heads out the door, I turn to Kate quickly, ready to ask before I lose my nerve. "Kate, that dance in your school - can anyone come? I mean, people who don't go to your school."

Kate nods immediately, as if she's been waiting for me to ask that question all this time. "Yeah."

I grin and stuff my hands in my pockets. "Well... Want to go with me?"

A smile spreads across Kate's face, and her green eyes sparkle the way they do when she's excited. "Yeah, totally!"

With that, the two of us head out the door and begin walking to Kate's house, Kate talking eagerly and me listening happily.

* * * * * * * * * *

On the night of the dance, I wait downstairs in Kate's living room, dressed in new clothes which I bought specifically for the occasion. Around six o'clock, Kate walks down the stairs, dressed in a knee-length green dress. Her reddish hair has been curled, and her face is lit up. She looks gorgeous.

Mr. Woodland snaps a couple photos with his Polaroid camera, and Mrs. Woodland gives her daughter a hug. "You look so pretty," she tells her.

I follow suit by repeating the words and give Kate the corsage I've been holding in my hand. Then, after Mr. Woodland takes a quick photo of the two of us, we're walking outside, shivering slightly in the night air.

Usually, I would be nervous to take a girl to a dance - but not now. Even though I've never been big on going to dances, and even though Kate is the first real girlfriend I've ever had, I feel comfortable with her. I feel as though I've known her for much longer than three months.

Although I feel confident now, though, this feeling begins slipping away as we get nearer to the school, and the peaceful quiet of the night disappears. As the school comes into view, we can hear music blasting and people talking.

"Well," says Kate as we approach the front door, "here we are. You ready?"

I nod and swallow hard, realizing how dry my mouth is. "Yeah."

I hold the door open for Kate. "It's in the gym," she yells over the loud music and chatter. "This way." She takes my hand and guides me through the crowded hallway until we've reached the gym.

I stare up at the ceiling and observe all the brightly colored streamers and disco ball spinning around, reflecting its light across the entire gym.

"Tim! Kate!" I come to attention and look around. Immediately, Scott and Jennifer come rushing over to us. Scott is wearing a suit that looks like mine, while Jennifer is wearing a pink dress and lots of makeup, visible even underneath her glasses. "You came!" yells Scott.

"Yeah," I say. That seems to be all I can really say at the moment.

"We wouldn't miss it!" exclaims Kate. "Hey, where are Susan and Charles'?"

"Still dancing. Susan hasn't stopped since she got here!" laughs Jennifer.

Hearing these words, Kate asks, "Wait, are they together?"

"Tonight, they are. She finally got him to ask her," answers Jennifer.

A new song begins playing, and the couple runs off, their energy far exceeding that of most other people in the gym.

I'm simply observing all the people when, out of the corner of my eye, I see Kate looking up at me. Turning to look at her, I raise my eyebrows. "What's up?"

Kate grins. "Wanna dance?"

I laugh. "Oh, yeah."

Still holding hands, the two of us walk over to the dance floor. An upbeat song is playing, and everyone is jumping around and singing. I'm barely jumping; I'm mostly watching Kate jump and laugh, her hair flying.

"Hey guys!" yells a familiar voice. Susan and Charles come running over and then continue to dance.

"Hey!" yell Kate and I at the same time.

"It's so loud," exclaims Kate, wincing a little.

"I know! Isn't it rad?" laughs Susan, staring up at her date, who's giving her a smile.

The four of us continue dancing until the song finishes. Then, Kate and I exit the dance floor and lean against the gym wall, breathless and laughing. "That was great," says Kate, pushing a loose strand of her curled, long hair out of her face.

I grin and nod. "Let's get some punch."

* * * * * * * * * *

A couple hours into the dance, another upbeat song is playing, and Kate is twirling and laughing. Suddenly, it ends - and the song, "Wonderful Tonight" by Eric Clapton begins. Kate slowly stops spinning and comes closer to me. Automatically, I take her in my arms, and we begin dancing, the mood changing just like that.

I've never slow danced with a girl before, but somehow, I know exactly what to do. Kate rests her head on my shoulder, and we dance in silence.

I get so wrapped up in the music that I'm startled when suddenly, Kate whispers, "Tim, I need to ask you something."

I whisper, "Okay."

What she says is something that I don't expect. "What do you think about us? I mean - oh, I don't know what I'm saying…"

"Um - us? I, uh, don't really know," I begin stammering, suddenly feeling nervous.

Kate lifts her head and stares into my eyes. She has never looked more beautiful. In fact, she's so beautiful that everything I'm trying to think of saying just flies out of my head. Then, before I know what's happening, she whispers, "I love you."

She loves me. Kate Woodland loves me. *Me.* My life has been turned upside-down more times than I can count, and I was never expecting any of the things that happened to me - but this has to be one of the most surprising things.

As we stare into each other's eyes, the world seems to freeze around us. I take a mental picture in my mind, promising myself that I'll remember every detail of the night: the bright colors, the flashing lights, the music - everything you would expect from a high school dance in the winter of 1986. But most of all, I'll always remember this moment with Kate. Just like that, I know what I need to say. Holding her close, I whisper, "I love you, too." Then, I lean forward slowly, and without quite knowing what I'm doing, I kiss the girl I love most in the world.

CHAPTER THIRTY-FIVE
MARK

Josh and I stop running once we reach the restaurant. Panting, we pause outside the door, trying to catch our breath. Then, we walk inside the building, scanning it for any sign of Steven. I expect to see him at the front counter. Instead, though, I end up seeing Davey.

"Hey, Mike -" he begins, but I interrupt him immediately.

"Where's Steven?" I ask.

Davey takes a moment to look back and forth at Josh and I. Then, with a confused look on his face, he says, "It's his day off. He's at home."

I swallow hard. "Where does he live?"

Davey scratches his head. "Well... he lives in an apartment a couple blocks away."

"Where?"

Seeing the desperate, determined look on my face, Davey turns and grabs a small piece of paper and a pen. He takes a moment to jot something down. Then, he hands it to me.

I scan the paper, take in the address, and nod. "Thanks, Davey."

Josh and I turn and run out the door - and we don't stop until we reach an apartment complex just about ten minutes away from the restaurant.

Slowing down, I examine each door carefully, trying to find Steven's apartment. However, to my surprise, Josh finds it first. "There it is," he exclaims, pointing at the door.

I nod and give Josh a pat on the shoulder. Then, we walk up to the door and press down on the intercom button leading to Steven's apartment.

"Hello?" a voice answers.

"Steven?" I say. "It's Mark. I've gotta talk to you."

There's silence for a moment. Then, I hear the telltale sound of the door buzzing and unlocking, and I hurry to open it.

Walking inside, Josh trailing just behind me, the two of us climb two flights of stairs before reaching Steven's apartment. I reach out to knock on the door but hesitate. I can feel myself losing my nerve.

"Mark?" says Josh - and suddenly, at the sound of his voice, I knock hard on the door. This is it - I can't go back now.

The door swings open almost immediately, and I find myself staring at Steven. He's wearing a white t-shirt and blue jeans, looking much more casual than usual. His eyes are wide with curiosity - but I pause to look at them only for half a second. Then, I avoid his gaze.

"Well… Come on in," he says, a hint of surprise in his voice.

I obey and walk inside, my head down and my hands stuffed in my pockets. Close behind me is Josh, who receives a warm smile from Steven. The three of us walk into the living room, where a small Christmas tree sits in the corner and a young woman is sitting on the couch .

"Uh, guys, you remember Erica, right?" says Steven, walking over to the girl. "You met her at the bowling alley."

I nod slowly, remembering the girl, and she gives me a soft smile, pushing her permed, black hair out of her face. "Hi," she says.

Erica then turns and gives Steven a questioning look. He takes a deep breath; the couple seems to be communicating through their thoughts. Then, his eyes land on me.

"So," he says, taking a seat on the couch, "you wanted to talk?"

I swallow hard. "Yeah." Then, I shift my gaze towards Josh and Erica.

Steven takes the hint and clears his throat. "Josh, um, why don't you go into the other room with Erica and check out my new book in there? It's really good, and it's sitting right on the nightstand - you won't miss it."

Erica puts a gentle hand on Josh's back to lead him away, and he nods - but the look he gives me tells me that he knows Steven and I want to talk by ourselves.

The moment Josh and Erica disappear into the bedroom, I turn to Steven and cross my arms. "Did you call the cops?"

Steven gapes at me and throws up his hands in frustration, as if he knew this was coming. "What? No!"

"Yes, you did. You knew about Josh and I, so you told them -"

"I didn't tell them a *thing*," says Steven, almost indignantly. "If you really knew how I felt, then you wouldn't even suggest that."

"Yeah, well, I *do* know how you feel," I snap. "I know exactly how you feel. If you cared, then you wouldn't have left."

Steven stares right at me, and a strange look comes over his face. It's a look of sadness, as if what I've said has wounded him. However, I ignore it.

"So? Why'd you call the cops?" I ask.

Steven shakes his head. His voice is quiet as he says, "A couple police officers came by the restaurant asking if I knew Josh. My guess is that someone in town recognized him from some 'missing person' ads, and they were the ones who reported him."

"What'd you say?"

"I just said that I knew him, but I hadn't seen him for a while. I said I had no idea where he was."

Steven looks so earnest as he says this that I almost believe him. Still, I'm not entirely convinced. "Did you really?"

"Yeah. And I was telling the truth. I didn't know where Josh was. I didn't know where you were, either."

"We left," I say quickly. "I thought you might turn us in."

Steven shakes his head and stares at me, a look of disappointment and confusion in his eyes. "Mark, why would I turn in my own brother?"

I feel as though I've been punched in the gut. All this time, I had a feeling - but I wasn't quite sure. Even when Steven told me he knew my name was Mark, I wasn't totally positive. Now, though, I know. I turn away and stare out the window, refusing to look at the face of my brother.

As if reading my thoughts, Steven sighs. "Come on, Mark," he says. "Look at me."

I'm so surprised at this that, slowly, I turn my head back towards him. My eyes wander up to look at his face - and I feel a shiver run down my spine.

Although the face is older, it's the same one I knew all those years ago, when I was just four years old. My memories from back then are just a blur, but I remember the day that my big brother Stevie left. He was only fifteen, but the look in his eyes told me he was much older. He gave me a hug and said, "You come by to see me, okay, champ? You'll come see me with Ma and Tim. Be a good boy for them, alright?" With that, my brother walked out the door - and that was it. He never came back.

It never hit me that my boss "Steven" and my brother "Stevie" were the same person. After all, I was only four years old when he left. I had completely forgotten what he looked like, and I had almost forgotten about him as a person;

I was taught not to talk about him or mention him at home. In time, I learned to forget about him.

Steven was the first person who ever abandoned me. I was just a little kid, and not entirely aware of the happy life that was slipping through my fingers. I didn't know that Steven had left because of our father. I didn't know that I'd never see my big brother again.

I used to wonder why he'd left and wished that he would come back and find me. I thought that, maybe, if Tim couldn't find me, then Steven would. One of my brothers was sure to come back for me and save me. One of them was sure to come - but they never did.

I feel my eyes begin to burn, and I wipe them with the back of my hand. Unable to catch my breath, I try breathing slowly, not wanting to have another panic attack. "Why did you leave?"

Steven looks down at his hands, and I can see something like hurt flash across his face. "Dad's drinking was out of control. It didn't used to be so bad - but he couldn't seem to get over the war. He wouldn't listen to anyone - not even Mom. So... I had to get out. And when I left, he told me to never come back. I moved in with my buddy from high school for a time."

I observe Steven's face. It's pale and stiff, as if he's trying hard not to let any emotion slip through and interrupt his story.

He takes a deep breath and continues. "Ma would come visit sometimes and give me some money when she had it. I missed her more than anything - and you and Tim, of course. But I couldn't see you."

I bite my lip, finally summoning up the courage to say what I've wanted to for years. "Okay. Well - even if you couldn't stay at home... Where were you when we needed you? When money was running out and we didn't know what we'd do, and then the accident?"

I take a few slow, deep breaths while Steven continues.

"I moved to Andersonville when I was eighteen. A couple years later, I read about the accident, and I went back to Charlotte to find you and Tim. I spoke with Child and Family Services, but they said I had no right to see you unless I had a court ordered document proving our relationship. Besides, I had no money for a lawyer and felt overwhelmed and hopeless. So... I had to come back here. And that was it."

Steven takes a deep breath and looks up at me, and I try to comprehend everything he's just told me. Looking at his face, now that I know who he really is, I can see a little bit of myself - but I can also see our dad... or, at least, the man our father used to be. The man I never really got to know, except through my mother's stories.

Steven isn't like our father. I know that now. But... I never got to forgive our father. Now, as I'm sitting across from my older brother, I realize that this is an opportunity to forgive someone else.

"How'd you know it was me?" I ask quietly. "How did you recognize me?"

Steven stares down at his lap. "Well… you look like Dad. And, besides, once Josh told me about your birthday, I was pretty sure it was you. Then, when I heard him call you Mark - that's when I knew for sure."

I nod. Then, suddenly, Steven looks up and exclaims, "Mark, I'm so sorry. You're my brother, and I wanted to find you and Tim - but it was impossible. I didn't have the money to take care of you, and I didn't even have the right to see you. I wasn't sure what to do. But now, you're here, and… I want to know if you can forgive me for leaving."

I stare at my hands and think about this for a moment. Can I forgive him? Can I even muster up enough courage to say the words? Even though I know that Steven isn't the one to blame, there's a deep wound inside me from the day he left. I don't think I can forgive him right away. But I want him to know how I feel - so I need to try.

Slowly, I shrug. "I think so."

CHAPTER THIRTY-SIX
MARK

There is a lot to sort through, and it isn't easy. I haven't talked to many people about the accident that killed my parents – the accident that was caused by my father drinking and driving. The one that I'm still dealing with the effects of to this day. The doctors and nurses told Tim and I that we were lucky to survive. It never felt lucky.

One hour later, after Steven and I have finished talking about the past, I remember the main reason that I came to talk to him. Quickly, I ask, "Steven - what do I do about the cops?"

Steven thinks for a moment. Then, he shakes his head. "You've gotta take Josh to the police, Mark."

I stand up suddenly. "What?"

"You need to take him to the police," repeats Steven. "You'll get in trouble if you don't."

"No," I mutter, beginning to pace back and forth.

Steven stands up, too. "Mark," he says firmly. "You'll be arrested."

I shake my head. "No, I won't. We'll run away."

"That's exactly what I'm talking about. You'll get arrested for kidnapping. You can't hide Josh forever."

"He doesn't want to go back there," I murmur, running my hands through my dark hair and walking around in a frenzy. "I can't take him there."

"They'll take you back to the foster home."

I stop walking suddenly. Turning around, I face Steven. The look on his face is firm - but there's concern in his eyes. "Bring him to the police station, and they won't ask questions. They came looking for Josh, not you. You're fourteen - but Josh is only seven. The police are more concerned about finding him."

I shake my head, trying desperately to get Steven to understand. "But -"

"Wherever they take him, he'll be *safe*, Mark. He's lucky he found you when he did - because you've been able to protect him. He may be smart, but he's just a little kid, Mark - and you're not an adult. You need to turn him in."

I stand there for a moment, breathing hard. I don't know what to do. I was so sure that the right place for Josh was with me... But all of a sudden, Steven's words seem to have a bit of reason in them.

"I don't know," I whisper. "He's... he's like..." I let my words trail off, unwilling to express to Steven just how much Josh means to me. I don't know how to tell him that Josh is like my little brother. I don't know how to tell him just how much it scares me to lose him.

Somehow, though, Steven seems to know exactly what I'm thinking. Laying a hand on my shoulder, he says,

"You've gotta let go, Mark. You need to do what's best for Josh."

Do what's best for Josh. Those words have been echoing in my head for days - and I thought I'd been listening to them this whole time. Now, though, I'm beginning to realize that I haven't. For some reason, I'm starting to think that Steven is right.

Suddenly, before I can open my mouth to reply, I hear a small voice ask, "What're you talking about?"

I whirl around to see that Josh has come out of the bedroom, with Erica standing just behind him. His small, skinny figure is hunched in a nervous sort of position, making me think that he heard much more of our conversation than I wanted.

"Josh," says Steven slowly, "the police have been looking for you. They want to take you back to the foster home."

"I know," whispers Josh. He looks much smaller than I've ever seen him before.

"Why are you afraid?" asks Erica gently, crouching down so that her eyes are level with Josh's. I'm surprised to hear her speak, but the look in her eyes tells me that Steven told her almost everything. At first glance, you wouldn't think of her as the motherly type - but the kind look on her face makes me think that it's a good idea to have her here right now. "What was so bad about that place?"

Josh shakes his head. "I'm not afraid. I ran away because I knew I'd never be adopted. I didn't want to stay there anymore - so I left. That was it. But…" Josh looks at me for a moment. Then, he says, "I'll go back."

I feel my jaw drop. "What?"

"I'll go back."

Steven's eyes widen in surprise. "Josh, are you sure?"

"Yes."

"Do you really mean it?" I ask. "B – because we could just -"

"I mean it," says Josh firmly. "I don't want you to get in trouble, Mark."

"I won't get in trouble, if I just -" I begin, but Steven interrupts me.

"Mark," is all he says - but I know what he's trying to tell me. He wants me to let Josh make the decision on his own.

"I'm ready to go," says Josh quietly, walking to the door.

I stay where I am, planted to the ground - but Steven pats my shoulder. "It's alright, brother," he whispers. "Remember: do what's best for him."

* * * * * * * * * *

Josh and I don't talk as we exit Steven's apartment. We walk for about ten minutes in silence, not quite sure which way to go. Then, I spot the police station in the distance. Josh seems to see it, too, because he begins walking a little faster.

I thought Josh would be afraid to turn himself in - but he doesn't seem to be. In fact, he seems determined to get there as soon as possible.

Suddenly, Josh looks up at me and asks, "Mark, are you coming with me?"

I raise my eyebrows. "Yeah. Of course, I am. Why do you ask?"

Josh hesitates. Then, he says, "Because... Well, you sounded scared inside Steven's apartment. I don't want you to get caught or anything."

"Nah," I say, patting Josh's back. "I'm not scared - and I'm not gonna get caught." I try to sound confident as I say this - but on the inside, I can't help feeling more anxious by the second.

Josh nods, looking much more confident than me. "You'll be okay, Mark. I know you will."

I shrug. "Well, I - I know that."

"But you've been kind of scared. I know that. And I know you didn't want to come back here, because of your brother. I just want to know..." Josh hesitates and searches my eyes before finishing his sentence, his voice softer than before. "When I turn myself in, and they take me back to the foster home... Well, are you just going to give up? Or are you going to find your brother?"

I glance down at my hands, hanging at my sides, and realize that they're shaking nervously. I grab my left wrist with my right hand, holding it tightly as though I can stop it from shaking.

"I - don't know." I say it quietly so that Josh can't notice the way my voice is shaking. "But - I do know that you're gonna be just fine. And it's not gonna be long before you're adopted. You're a good kid. I know you'll get a family soon. I know you will."

"Come on, Mark - will you promise me?" begs Josh, unwilling to be diverted from the topic.

Silence. I stare off into the distance, thinking hard about what to say. The world seems to move in slow motion as I wait, and I watch as a few drops of rain begin to fall from the darkening sky.

"I won't give up," I answer finally. "I promise. If I know you'll be okay, then I'll be okay, too."

A grin appears on Josh's freckled face, and he nods. "Good." Then, the two of us start walking again, headed towards the police station and towards the next stage of our lives.

* * * * * * * * * *

My heart starts beating faster and faster as Josh and I approach the police station. The door is thirty seconds ahead of me... then twenty... then ten.

I stop at the sidewalk across the street. "I can't go in there, Josh. They'll send me back. I can't let that happen now."

Josh nods. Kneeling so that we're eye-level, I stare right into his eyes and say quietly, "I've gotta go."

A panicked look appears on Josh's face, and he shakes his head. "No! Not yet!"

I blink in surprise. I've never known Josh to be this distressed. "I have to, Josh. You've gotta go back now, and…" I lower my voice so that only he can hear me. "I can't risk gettin' caught or anything like that. You know how it is."

"But… I didn't think you'd have to go right away." Right now, Josh is looking and acting more like a little boy than he ever has before - and it worries me.

"No, Josh. I have to go. And you need to go back - you said so yourself. Please, just trust me. I wouldn't be leaving you like this if I didn't believe that you'd be happy. And - I'll be happy, too. So, you don't need to worry about me."

Josh nods slowly, his eyes still focused on me. "Will you write to me, Mark?"

"Sure, I will. I don't have a return address, though."

Josh bites his lip, considering this. "Well… Please talk to your brother."

I shrug and glance over my shoulder in a sudden attempt to change the subject. "I gotta go, Josh."

As soon as I've said those four words, I watch Josh's eyes fill up again and flow over. "M - Mark. D - don't leave me yet, p - please."

I shake my head firmly, even though my own chest feels tired and heavy now, as if I've been crying like Josh. "You'll be just fine, Josh; you'll have people looking after you now. And trust me - you need them more than you need me." The words spill out of my mouth before I can stop them. Suddenly, I wish I hadn't even said them - because part of me doesn't truly believe myself.

"B - but I just want y - you," sobs Josh, his tears making paths through the dirt on his face. Suddenly, he throws his arms around me, and I hold him, unable to think about anything except the fact that this scared little boy can't be the confident kid I was talking to just a few minutes ago.

"It's okay," I find myself whispering in a soothing, gentle voice that isn't my own. "It's all gonna be okay."

"W - what if I n - never see you again?" cries Josh, his voice hiccupping.

"You will see me again. You will. Hey, it's okay, Josh." I loosen my grip on the little boy and hold him by the shoulders. "You've gotta be brave. For me. Okay?"

Although tears are still running down his face, Josh nods and rubs his eyes. "O - okay."

Part of me wants to stay right where I am instead of leaving. That part is because I can guess how Josh is feeling right now - and I don't want him to feel abandoned by me, the way I felt when Steven left years ago, and then when Tim didn't come back for me. I don't want Josh to grow up with that constant feeling of loss, the way I have. But the way Josh is standing there, ready to head back to the foster home and maybe be adopted sometime soon - well, to keep him from going might just ruin his life. And I can't do that.

Standing up, I begin walking down the sidewalk, trying to force myself to leave. Josh does the same and takes a few steps towards the police station. Then, suddenly, Josh whirls around and runs to me, wrapping his arms around my waist. "I love you, Mark. D - don't forget about me."

I feel as though I'm going to choke, and I let Josh hug me for only a second. Then, I pull back and nod. "I promise. I'll never forget about you, Josh."

With one last look at me, Josh sniffs, wipes his eyes, and walks across the street. After a moment, he disappears inside the police station. Then, I turn away - and I start running.

CHAPTER THIRTY-SEVEN
TIM

Somehow, today is Christmas Eve - and I'm not totally sure that I can comprehend it. I wake up to sunlight filtering through my window, and I lay in bed for a long time, unable to accept the fact that for the fourth time in a row, I'm going to be spending the holiday without my family.

Around eleven o'clock, I exit the YMCA, wearing a warm jacket over my regular clothes. My first instinct is to go see Kate, like I've been doing every day that she's been home for winter break - but I don't feel like being with her right away. Kate invited me to spend the evening with her family, and I accepted eagerly. However, when I said yes, I didn't expect to be in the kind of mood I'm in today.

Walking through the streets of Davidson, it's easy to tell that it's Christmas, thanks to the fact that practically every shop is decorated with colorful, twinkling lights. Wreaths hang on shop doors, and big bells with red ribbons hang at the tops of the door frames. Some shops even have small trees sitting in their windows.

I used to love Christmas. I still do. But it's a *new* kind of Christmas - the kind that's spent with my girlfriend and her family, and not with my own. I thought I would be used to that by now, but I'm not. This past month, the closer we got to Christmas, the angrier I felt - angry at myself, angry at the world, and angry at the people who've kept my brother and I apart for so long.

Eventually, I exit the downtown part of Davidson and enter Kate's neighborhood. Glancing through some windows, I can see families gathered, spending time with one another. I swallow hard as I reach far into my memory, trying to think of some sort of happy memory I have from a Christmas long ago. Although I know the memories do exist, it's hard for me to bring them to mind. All I can think about are the versions of my family that I last saw - the versions that will exist in my mind forever.

There was our father, shattered on the inside and out and fighting to keep going, sometimes showing us glimpses of the man he used to be - the man he was before he was drafted in the Vietnam War; our mother, just trying to take care of her sons and love them enough for two people; Mark, a boy rebellious and full of fire; me, an outsider just trying to be a good son and brother; and then, there was Steven. Yeah - there was another of us. Our oldest brother.

Never was there a time that I didn't think of *myself* as the oldest son. It wasn't that I didn't know that Steven existed; it was because he was never around. He left when I was just a kid, and as soon as he was gone, I made it my own personal priority to make sure that I was a good big brother to Mark.

I remember the way Steven would play with us when we were just little kids - but as soon as he left, I knew that those good times had ended. He was so much older than me that we had never been able to see life the same way, or truly understand each other on a deeper level - but I do remember what he said to me the day he left.

Our dad wasn't at home that day, and we stood with our mother at the apartment door to say goodbye, Steven bent down to talk to me.

"Tim, I'm gonna see you again," he said, his eyes wide and serious as he held my shoulders with both hands. Back then, he had looked so old to me - but when I remember him now, I just see a scared-looking fifteen-year-old trying to be braver than he was. "Ma will bring you over sometimes, and we'll play games, just like always. It'll be fun. You bring some card games over, alright?"

I nodded, pushing my dirty-blond hair out of my eyes. "O - okay."

"I - I won't be coming back here, so I'm gonna need you to be the oldest brother. Okay, Tim? Always take care of Mom and Mark for me. I know you can."

I nodded again, watching the way Steven's eyes suddenly filled up with tears. Just like that, I was swept up into a hug, and I squeezed my big brother tightly. I didn't fully understand what was going on, and at the same time - well, somehow, I knew.

That was back when I was young enough to refrain from being bitter against my brother, but old enough to feel like the weight of the world was on my shoulders. Just like that, my big brother, the one who was supposed to be taking care of our mom and Mark and I, shifted all his responsibility to me. He did it too soon.

It was too much, as I quickly found out - and by the time I was eleven, I was sure I resented him for it. Only eleven years old, and I was already an adult. Maybe my friends didn't see me that way, and maybe even my family didn't see me that way, but it was the way I felt. I felt like I'd never had a childhood, and it was all Steven's fault. I never wanted to see him again, so I didn't. And then, just like that, I lost everyone and everything I'd ever known.

I never blamed Mark for anything that ever happened to me. I could never do that. He was just a kid; he was the little brother I'd practically raised. But Steven... Now, he was someone I could blame. And so was our dad. So, as it turned out, the two men in my family that I should've been able to look up to ended up being the two people who I blamed for the terrible things that happened in my life. The trouble is, I'm still blaming them - and I don't know how I can forgive them.

Suddenly, I hear someone call my name. "Tim!"

I look to my left and realize that I'm standing in front of Kate's house. She's rushing down the front steps, her hair tied back in a high ponytail. She's not wearing a coat, causing me to believe that she doesn't plan to be outside for long.

Shivering, she walks up to me, her arms crossed. "Merry Christmas."

I force a smile. "Merry Christmas."

As if the very words have caused the weather to jump into action, I notice that a few snowflakes are beginning to fall. My eyes follow them through the air, and I see that Kate has noticed them too. Her green eyes are sparkling in excitement, and she holds out her hand, trying to catch a few. Although a few land on her hand, they melt quickly, while the ones that land on her reddish hair stick a couple seconds longer.

"So," says Kate quietly, motioning for us to sit in the white wicker chairs on her front porch, "what're you doing?"

I shrug and sit down. "I don't know. Well... I'm just thinking, I guess."

Kate looks over at me and tilts her head. "About what?"

I say the first thing that pops into my head. "Christmas."

Kate laughs. "Aren't we all?"

I grin - but it's not even close to genuine. Kate must notice this because the smile on her face disappears almost instantly. "Tim? Are you okay?"

Suddenly nervous, I nod quickly. "Yeah, of course I am." Then, trying to be lighthearted, I raise my eyebrows and ask, "Are you?"

Kate nods slowly. Then, to my surprise, I notice the way Kate's cheeks flush, and her eyes begin to water.

"Kate," I say suddenly, "what's wrong?"

"Nothing," says Kate quietly. "It's just… Well, it's silly, and I don't expect you to understand."

"Come on," I reply. "Try me."

Kate bites her lip. Then, she says, "I just… I'm so used to being with my family, you know? I mean, I guess I never expected things to change, so I never planned for my life to be any different. But…"

Kate hesitates, and I raise my eyebrows. "Yes?"

Sighing, Kate looks up at me and shakes her head. "I just don't feel ready to leave my family."

"To leave them?"

Kate's eyes shift quickly to stare down at the ground. "I meant to tell you before, but I never got around to it. I guess I just assumed that you'd already - well."

"What is it?" I ask, feeling much more worried than I look.

"I'm a senior in high school, Tim. I'm graduating in the spring. And I never used to think that I'd go to college. My parents graduated college, and they wanted me to go, too, but with them already helping pay for Andy's tuition… Well, I don't think any of us even considered the possibility - at least not right away. Then, a few weeks ago, I…"

I nod to urge her to continue.

Kate sighs and bites her lip in hesitation. Then, quickly, she says, "I got a scholarship. To a school in California."

It takes everything in me to keep my jaw from literally dropping. "What? You did?"

"Mhm. I promise, I was going to tell you before, but - I guess I kept putting it off."

"A school in California. *California.* Have you ever even been there, Kate?"

Kate shrugs. "Well, no. But I know it's warm."

"Yeah, I'm sure it is."

"Please say you're happy for me, Tim," she exclaims suddenly, obviously sensing the subtle sharpness in my words.

Seeing the mix of worry, hurt, and sadness in her eyes, I take her hand quickly and switch my frame of mind in half a second. "Of course, I'm happy! Why wouldn't I be? I mean, a scholarship? That's - that's awesome! It's really great. I mean, it's fantastic. Of course, you got a scholarship; you're the smartest person I know. You're -"

"Terrified. I'm terrified." Kate's eyes well up with tears, and mine widen at the mere sight of it. I've truly never seen Kate so openly afraid.

"Why? This is probably the best opportunity you've ever had in your life," I say, keeping my voice soft and calm.

"'Best opportunity I've ever had.' That's what everyone keeps telling me. But I don't believe it. I *can't* believe it. Why would I want to leave my life behind while I move thousands and thousands of miles away?"

I shake my head. "Kate, that's crazy. You can't go through life thinking about what you're leaving behind. Especially when you'll come back to it one day."

A single tear rolls down Kate's cheek, a few snow-flakes mixing with it. "B - but will I?"

I frown. "What're you talking about?"

"It's not just my family who I'm going to miss, you know." She doesn't have to say anything more. I know what she means.

"Don't be like that. Please, don't turn down this op-portunity because of *one person*."

"Tim, I'm telling you, that one person means so much to me that I'd be willing to turn *anything* down if it meant I could stay with him."

Just like that, before I can do or say anything, she leans forward and kisses me. It's enough to distract me for a few seconds - but once it's over, I just shake my head. "I'm not enough for you to give up everything for me. You de-serve everything. I've known that ever since I met you, and I've known it for a long time now. For once in your life, do something for *yourself*."

"So, what are you saying?" exclaims Kate. "Are you saying that you'll - that you'll still be here? Waiting for me?"

I nod firmly. "Yes."

"But - why?"

I hesitate before answering. "Well, for more than one reason. The first one is because of what I said before. You deserve everything - and you don't deserve to be left behind just because you decide to pursue your dream. I'm always gonna be here for you. And the second reason is - well, I wanna be here for someone else. Someone who needs me just as much as I need him."

Kate nods for a second, and then she moves closer to me and rests her head on my shoulder. "Thank you."

CHAPTER THIRTY-EIGHT
TIM

Christmas Day came and went quickly. I spent part of the day with Kate's family, and the other by myself. The day passed by in a similar way to Christmas Eve, except that I'd had a little more time to process my feelings about the holiday - and my feelings about Kate's announcement.

Now, it's New Year's Eve, and I'm preparing to spend the evening at Kate's house. Apparently, her parents throw a party every year, and practically everyone they know is invited. Thankfully, this means that I'll know quite a few people, so I won't feel totally out of place.

Around six o'clock, I head over to Kate's house, dressed in a blue sweater and tan pants, with my warm jacket on for good measure. Walking up to the front step, I don't hesitate to knock on the door, eager to get out of the cold.

As soon as the door swings open, I'm surprised to find myself looking not at Kate, but at her brother Andy.

"Hey, man!" he greets me, patting me on the back as I step inside. "Come on in. Good to see you."

I grin and return the greeting. The door shuts behind me, and Andy leads me over to the living room.

Warm light is flooding the house, making it hard for my eyes to adjust. When they do, I find myself standing amid over twenty people, all dressed extra nicely in honor of the occasion. Music is blasting, and I recognize the song as "1999" by Prince.

I take a moment to search the room for Kate. It's hard for me to locate her among the brightly colored balloons and many people - but eventually, I spot her. She's deep in conversation with Susan and their friend Jennifer. I pause at the edge of the room for a moment, simply to observe her.

She's so beautiful. That's not all I love about her, of course - because it's her joy that *makes* her beautiful. Light is radiating on her face, and she can't seem to stop smiling - and I love her for it.

After I've been standing for a moment, I decide to get her attention. I give her a little wave, and her eyes land on me. Immediately, they light up, and she says a few words to Susan and Jennifer before rushing over.

"Hi," she says eagerly, smoothing out her green sweater and jeans.

"Hey," I reply. "You look beautiful."

I don't hesitate in saying this anymore. I don't hesitate in *anything* anymore - because I know how I feel. I know how I feel about Kate, and everything else. I know that I need to tell her exactly how I feel from now on... even if I'm going to have to say goodbye in just a few months.

Kate blushes and takes my hand. "Thanks." Then, she leads me into the crowd, where I spend the next hour or so talking to various people. Some I know, and some I don't - but all seem friendly and welcoming. The music is playing loudly, everyone's happy, and before I know it, it's time to watch the ball drop on television.

Kate and I stand next to each other by the living room window as the countdown begins. The entire group at the party begins counting along with the people in Times Square. "Three... Two... One... Happy New Year!"

As everyone begins talking excitedly, Kate and I turn to each other.

"Happy New Year," she whispers.

I smile. Instead of replying, I lean forward and kiss my girlfriend - the girl that I love. Our eyes are closed as we embrace for a moment. A few moments later, I glance out the window - and my eyes land on a tall, familiar figure walking down the sidewalk.

I can't see the person's face clearly - but at that moment, a strange feeling comes over me. I don't know what it is, but I can't stay inside a second longer. I have to go outside and talk to that person.

Pulling away from Kate, I give her a smile and a gentle nudge, signaling to her that she should go talk to some of the guests. She walks away, and I slip away towards the front door.

It's started snowing lightly, making it harder to see outside in the darkness. Still, even as I approach the stranger, I have a feeling that I've met them before. In fact, I'm so sure of this that I take a chance and call out the name that's been waiting on my lips. "Mark."

He stops suddenly. He's past the house by now, but I know he hears me. He glances over his shoulder, his eyes landing on me immediately. I start walking towards him; he doesn't run. So, I start walking faster. By the time I've reached him, he's turned around fully and is simply staring at me.

Up close, I can notice things about my brother that I didn't before. For one, he's practically my height at this point. His eyes are slightly bloodshot, and there are dark circles around them, indicating that he must be exhausted. He looks even older than the last time I saw him, and there's a strange sort of look on his face - a look of sadness... Maybe even more. It's a look of... *hopelessness*.

"Mark?" I say again, except this time, it's more of a question.

He nods slowly but doesn't say anything.

I take a deep breath and shake my head. "What are you doing here?"

Mark stares down at the sidewalk, where a few snowflakes have begun to stick. "I... Well... I asked around, and I found out you might be here. So... I came."

I can feel my heart begin to soar. This is a completely different version of Mark than I saw last time. Last time, he was hostile and angry; this time, he's barely even raised his voice.

"Why?" I ask quietly. "Why'd you wanna find me?"

Mark swallows hard. Then, he shrugs and looks away. "I don't know. Why'd you come outside?"

I throw my hands up in desperation. "What do you mean, why'd I come out here? Because I saw my *brother*! Mark, you may never understand why I went looking for you, and you might always be angry at me for not having done it sooner. I mean, I'm not a mind reader; I don't know exactly how you're feeling right now. All I know is, the only thing I want is for you and I to be a family again. Maybe you were scared, and maybe I was, too. But all that can change. Why should we be afraid of things going back to the way they were?"

Mark scoffs. "That's the dumbest question I've ever heard."

I sigh and rub my hand over my face. He's not wrong. The lives we lived in Charlotte as kids weren't the best that we could've had.

"Okay, sure. What I mean is… Why can't we be a family again?"

Mark opens his mouth as if he wants to say something, but he hesitates. After a moment of silence, he begins to talk. "Tim… I learned to stop trusting people a long time ago. So, when you say you want us to be a family again… Well, how am I supposed to believe that?"

"'Cause I really mean it," I say firmly. "I know you've got no reason to trust me. I know that you've been hurt more than once. I was hurt, too. I'm not good at forgiving people. But I know that's the best thing I could do.

We're supposed to forgive people no matter what, even if they don't deserve it - you know?"

Mark shrugs. "Sounds like one of Ma's old sayings from her book or somethin'."

I bite my lip. "It's called 'the Bible,' Mark. And yeah - that's where the idea comes from. Point is, I'm not doing such a good job at forgiving people - but I'm trying. And I'm trying to make up for all the things I've done wrong in my life, like not going back for you right away. So, I figure if I'm trying to forgive people, then why don't you try, too? We can learn together."

Mark sighs and folds his arms across his chest. "Seems a little late for that. To forgive people, I mean."

I shake my head. "Are you kidding? Now's the time to tell people you forgive 'em... 'cause... you might not get to one day."

I notice the way Mark's expression changes suddenly at these words. That's when I decide to ask one more time.

"Mark," I say, my voice barely above a whisper, "can't we be a family again?"

Suddenly, as I stare at my younger brother, his straight, stoic face begins to change. He bites his lip, and his eyes squeeze shut for a moment, and just like that, he's *crying*. Mark, my tough, serious kid brother, is crying. "Yeah," he whispers shakily, reaching up to wipe the few tears that are running down his cheeks. "I think so."

I stand there for a moment, unable to comprehend what's happening. Then it hits me, and I step forward and grab my younger brother, wrapping him in a hug. The dream I thought would never come true is unfolding before my eyes. After almost four years, my brother and I are together again. *Finally,* I think to myself, staring up gratefully at the dark sky above us. *Finally.*

EPILOGUE
MARK

Back in the year 1983, I never would have imagined my life the way it is now. I could never have foreseen the challenges that my brothers and I would face, and the struggles we would go through. No one wants to go through hard things - but now, as I look back on the past five years, I realize that they taught me some important things.

A lot happened after my older brother and I reunited on New Year's Day, 1987. For starters, once Tim took me to stay with him in his room at the YMCA, I told him about Steven.

To my surprise, Tim was scared. I'd never seen him like that before, and I asked him what was wrong. What he said surprised me. He told me that, just like how I had struggled to forgive Tim, he was struggling to forgive Steven.

I convinced Tim to go see Steven with me, and he agreed. So, on January 2nd, we went to see Steven at his apartment.

When our older brother opened the door, his face became so white, he looked as though he was going to faint. Then, he wrapped Tim in a hug - a sure sign that us three Ryder brothers were going to be together from now on.

As the three of us settled in at Steven's apartment, he began to prepare for a legal battle to win custody over me. Tim would be eighteen in a month, and therefore didn't need a legal guardian anymore - but I would need one for a few more years.

The process was long and messy. It forced us brothers to dive deep into our past - an experience too painful for us to talk about with one another. Eventually, though, just as the summer came to an end, Steven was granted custody over me, and us brothers were allowed to live together. It was what should have happened years ago, and to finally be together again lifted a large weight off our shoulders.

Each of us in turn had his own unique experience during that year, and the one to follow it. Steven decided to get his GED, since he never finished high school. He worked during the day and went to night school after that, determined to earn his diploma. He loved reading more than ever, and he told me that he wanted to learn to write just like the authors of the books he read - although for now, he would focus on developing his culinary skills.

Around this time, he and his girlfriend Erica became more serious. She visited the apartment often and talked a lot with Tim and I, wanting to get to know us better. Eventually, she almost seemed to be part of the family. It wasn't long before Tim and I learned that she *was* going to be part of the family, when Steven proposed to her on May 20th, 1988.

Tim faced a difficult situation when August of 1987 came around. One day, he drove with his girlfriend and her family to the airport. He came back a couple hours later, alone. In his hand was an envelope which he clutched tightly. I asked what it was, but he shook his head, and with a faint smile on his face, he told me it was nothing. I didn't ask any more questions - but I did quickly notice that he was racking up a lot of long-distance phone bills.

That month, Tim also went back to school. He went through his senior year just one year late and graduated with flying colors. I was proud of him. Since then, he's been very busy with work and his college classes. Although he comes home tired every day, he seems to get a lot of satisfaction out of school - a feeling I can't exactly relate to.

As for me, I spent the summer of 1987 getting reacquainted with my brothers and trying to figure out what to do with my life. I hadn't been to school in a long time, and I wasn't sure I was ready to go back. Both of my brothers encouraged this, though, so I eventually gave in and went into my eighth-grade year of school. Thankfully, once I neared high school the next year, my teachers allowed me to take summer school to catch up, which landed me as a sophomore right when I should have been.

Being at school helped distract me from my troubles - and it eventually went as far as to cure me from my headaches. Some leftover symptoms from the crash still haunt me to this day, but they aren't as strong. Sometimes, I'm even able to forget about them for a while.

Today is June 21st, 1990. One year ago exactly, I sat next to Tim and Kate at Steven and Erica's wedding reception. The newlyweds were moving from table to table, guest to guest, beaming and unable to stop looking into each other's eyes. It was easy to see how much they loved one another.

The two of them drove to Virginia Beach for their honeymoon and stayed for just a few days, having to get back home quickly so Steven could get back to his job as a short-order cook at one of Andersonville's finest restaurants, and Erica back to her job as an English teacher at the local elementary school. Now, they've been happily married for a whole year, and all of us are gathered in the living room of our small house.

"So," asks Tim, "what's up, guys?"

Steven raises his eyebrows innocently. "What do you mean?"

Tim grins. "Well, you called a family meeting. What's going on?"

"Well," says Erica, leaning forward and letting her black hair fall over her shoulders, "we've got a surprise for you guys."

I widen my eyes. "What is it?"

Erica looks at Steven, and the two of them take each other's hands and exchange a smile. Then, Steven says, "Well... We've decided to expand our family. We're going to adopt."

I can feel my jaw drop open. I glance over at Tim and notice a similar look of astonishment on his face. "What?" he exclaims. "But..." He hesitates.

Steven frowns. "What?"

"Well… It just seems like you haven't been married that long. I mean… Do you really feel ready to adopt a baby?"

Steven sighs and nods. "Tim, I'm twenty-eight, and so is Erica. We've been married an entire year, and we don't see any reason to wait any longer. We're going to adopt."

I grin. Although I'm shocked, I don't see any problem with the idea. "Good for you, guys."

Steven looks over at me suddenly. "Mark… There's something else that we haven't told you. We're not adopting a baby."

I tilt my head in confusion. "What? A kid, then?"

"Josh."

The name hits me so hard that I practically fall back onto the couch. The little boy and I have been writing to each other for years, ever since we had to say goodbye. He's ten now, while I'm seventeen, and although we haven't been able to see one another in person for a long time (thanks to the visitation rules), I still feel like his older brother.

"Josh," I echo. "You mean… Josh? Like, *the* Josh?"

Erica laughs. "Yes," she says. "Steven and I have already made plans to pick him up next month. We started the adoption process immediately after our wedding, but we didn't want to get anyone's hopes up."

My head begins spinning, and I wring my hands anxiously - something I haven't done in a long time. "You mean - he'll be here? He'll be -"

"Our nephew," grins Tim. Suddenly, the concern that was on his face just a moment ago disappears, and now, all I can see is excitement. Our family, which survived as just three brothers for so long, is growing magically before our eyes.

"Yeah," I breathe. "Our nephew."

* * * * * * * * * *

On August 15th, around three o'clock, Tim and I wait in the living room, anticipating Josh's arrival. I've been waiting impatiently for this day to come, and now that it's here, I'm not totally sure how I feel. I know I'm excited, but I also know that I'm nervous. What will Josh be like? Will he be happy to see me?

The moment Tim and I see Steven and Erica pull into the driveway, I notice the car door swing open, and I see a flash of red hair. Opening the front door and rushing out, I run to the car and find myself standing in front of Josh.

He's almost eleven now, and at least a foot taller since I saw him last. His face is older, and he's less bony looking. He looks surprised, even though he must have known that I was going to be here. Above all, though, he looks happy.

"Hey, Josh," I say hesitantly, not quite sure how to talk to him anymore. I'm going into my senior year of high school, while Josh is going into his fifth-grade year of elementary school. I'm not a kid anymore - and he doesn't appear to be much of one, either. We're both different.

"Hey, Mark," he replies in a slightly deeper voice that doesn't seem to belong to him.

I swallow hard. I can feel Tim's presence over my shoulder. He never held back his feelings from me when we reunited three years ago. He showed me how much he cared about me. Now that I'm in his shoes, I'm going to follow his lead.

"Man, I missed you," I say, laughing despite the growing lump in my throat.

Josh smiles - and as soon as he does so, its familiarity brings me so much joy that I step forward and give Josh a hug. Tim is next to welcome him, shaking his hand and telling him how excited he is to meet him. The next thing I know, we're walking inside the house, along with Steven and Erica - *Josh's parents*.

Sitting in that living room, in that little brick house on August 15th, 1990, I'm not quite sure what to think about life anymore. You can't expect anything that's going to happen in life - you just have to let it surprise you. Sometimes, those surprises are hard to take - but it's the way that you deal with them that matters. The important thing is that no matter what happens, you can always have faith. I glance at Tim and smile as my eyes fill with gratitude, remembering the words he has uttered a thousand times: "Therefore, I have hope."

ACKNOWLEDGMENTS

This story has been three years in the making. With everything from sibling bonds to romance to a nostalgic undercurrent, the book you have just read was drawn from a desire inside me to write a story full of hope in every circumstance. There were times when I wasn't sure I would be able to share this book with the world, but thanks to every person who helped me through the process, it is now available to you – the reader. Thank you for letting me share this story with you.

Now, to thank all the many people who helped this book reach its full potential and took the time to give me much-appreciated love, feedback, and support!

To Mom and Dad: You two are my first (and best) cheerleaders, and I'm so incredibly grateful to you for everything you've poured into this book. You're two of my first readers, my editors, my critique partners, and most importantly, my parents. I love you!

To my sister, Ivy: My first reader and one of my biggest helpers. I'm so thankful for all the help you gave me, including giving me an important plot twist. Your feedback and opinions are so valuable to me, and I love you!

To all my family: Without your love and support, I wouldn't be releasing this book into the world. Ever since I first said I wanted to be an author at the age of four, you've continually encouraged me and given me the inspiration I need to continue writing. Love you!

To my amazing beta readers: From the moment you agreed to beta read for me, you never failed to give me honest, thorough feedback. You truly made me feel like the book was coming together; thank you so much for your friendship!

To all my friends: The encouragement each of you has given me during this process is amazing! Whether you knew a lot about the book or very little, you always shared in my excitement and asked how the book was coming along. Thank you!

To the One who gave me this book, who inspired the story and gave me the message of hope I wanted to convey. Thank You for always being with me and showing me that You are in control.